The boy sat alone in the back of the class with his hood on. No teacher or student paid much mind to him, he rarely turned in assignments but was too smart to fail any classes. The boy didn't need human interaction, his thoughts and daydreams were enough to keep him satiated. On the first day of high school the prettiest girl in school had taken a picture with him. The boy thought it had been a miracle as he had always adored her from a distance, but his hopes and dreams were crushed only moments later. He was scrolling through Facebook when he noticed her picture with him posted under the caption "first day of school- befriend the school shooter" with several laughing emojis.

The incident stung obviously, but the pain melted away once he realized that this was just how things had always been and how they always would be. The boy had read several books about the psychology of the criminal mind, and knew that he showed no signs of a potential "school shooter". Besides, the boy knew in his gut that he could never hurt another living soul. People were too interesting. He believed they had too much potential to put the fire of their souls out. Death was something that came all too soon he thought, as he remembered his cousin Michael.

Michael had been a role model in the young boy's life until a couple of years ago. After struggling with addiction for years, he finally succumbed to a heroin overdose and died in his bed at the young age of twenty-two.

"What a shame." The boy's Mother had said.

"How awful, a waste of such great potential." His Father had said.

The boy had nothing to say about the incident. All he remembered from the funeral was the sobbing of his Aunt, and his Uncle staring into the distance. The man was looking at nothing it appeared. Perhaps he had been trying to stare into that black void that had taken Michael away from him. Whatever his uncle had been staring at, the young boy knew that he had never found what he was looking for. His Uncle would never again see his son, the boy he had raised into a man. Never again would he embrace Michael or take his keys after a long night of drinking. Never again watch as Michael built snowmen with his young cousin.

The boy remembered that day with sadness and misunderstanding. He never understood why such a great person could fall into a trap like drugs. Why such a smart person would make one stupid decision after another. He never understood why the universe had decided Michael's flame was to be extinguished at such a young age.

As the boy sat in the back of the class observing the people around him, several oddities began to confront him. First off, why was Jess quite obviously trying to give Adam a handjob under the table? Everyone knew Adam was gay. Adam had flirted with the boy every day since middle school. The second thought that raced through his mind was why had Adam always been so nice to him? Besides the whole gay thing,—which never really mattered to the boy—Adam was a very popular kid. He threw house parties once a month and always invited the boy. Of course the boy had never taken Adam up on the invites. After all, who wanted the school shooter to show up to a party?

As the boy looked around the room he noticed the teacher working a math problem out on the board. Mr. Jensen had no business being at the front of the classroom, only a teaching certificate which allowed it, and clearly couldn't explain anything about trigonometry that wasn't already explained in the book.

"What a waste of a life," thought the boy. What had happened in this poor man's past that had forced him to teach a bunch of snobby rich public school kids from Orange County? The more he pondered Mr. Jensen's background the more intrigued he became. What else did this man do with his time? Why would a well-spoken man in his twenties end up teaching algebra? Had the real world been so cold to him that he reverted back to high school? Perhaps he was one of the popular kids in high school, hadn't made it much further than that, and eventually decided to go back to where his glory days were.

Moving on past the obviously dim-witted man at the front of the classroom, the boy stopped to stare at one of the walls. It was filled with all kinds of geometric shapes and trigonometric functions.

"Ridiculous." the boy mused as he scanned the *Real World Applications for Arithmetic*. One of the applications was for a bakery. How you could track your income of loaves and the profit margin from their sales. Who the fuck would ever want to end up working in a bakery for the rest of their life?

It was easy for the boy to be critical. Never in his life had he set a goal or destination for himself. In kindergarten his teacher had asked each member of the class what they wanted to be when they grew up. Most of the children gave boring and typical answers. The girl who still couldn't comprehend two plus two wanted to be a doctor. The boy who was constantly throwing woodchips at other kids wanted to be a policeman. When asked what he wanted to be when he grew up, the young boy with no goals said he wanted to be a bird. Both the class and teacher had laughed hysterically at the notion.

"What was wrong with being a bird?" the boy thought. They can go wherever they want, never have to worry about the stupidity of others, and didn't really have to socialize. Plus he could poop on people. That would be awesome.

Now that he was a teenager the boy still had no idea what he wanted to be when he grew up. Obviously being a bird was out of the question. Maybe he would be a pilot, which seemed like the closest thing to being a bird. Or maybe he would become a traveling mystic man. The boy had read plenty of books describing shaman and medicine men. They were revered in many eastern Asian cultures. He couldn't speak a word of Mandarin, but that didn't matter much to him.

Even at a young age the boy had been entranced by dreams. Not the dreams of common peasants or of luxury or fame. The boy had always dreamed of freedom. True freedom. Walking the earth with nothing but a backpack. Lately his dreams had become tinted by the terrifying aspect of control. He had done his research on lucid dreaming and understood that it was a normal occurrence in most people. But when he was in control of his dreams five nights out of the week, he began to worry that soon he would never again be able to slip into the soft embrace of a dream to take him off on whatever adventure the night had in store for him.

The bell pulled him out of the trance he had fallen into, so the boy packed up his bag and began to lead the way out the door.

"Mr. Rivera," chimed a voice from behind him. The boy turned to see Mr. Jensen staring at him with what appeared to be the latest test in his hands.

"Mr. Jensen, what's up?" Asked the boy.

"Would you mind staying after for just a minute, I'd like to go over your test with you."

"Umm yeah, sure." He replied with a grimace. "I'd love nothing more."

As the boy trudged back towards the desk Mr. Jensen seemed to notice his apparent disdain at being held late.

"Got a hot date you were running off to?" inquired the man.

"Actually yeah, your mom's waiting for me out back, so if we could hurry this up that'd be great." The boy stated, with as much sarcasm towards the simpleton as he could muster.

Mr. Jensen's face shot into a smile instantly. Not what the boy had expected. Most teachers were boring unsophisticated prats who didn't understand or tolerate the boy's humor. Perhaps it was because Mr. Jensen was younger. Maybe it was because he knew his mother was a milf just as much as the rest of the senior class did.

"So tell me something Jake," the teacher started, "how is it that you manage to do almost no homework for my class, but still maintain the highest average test scores out of all four periods?"

"Well sir, I like to think I'm smarter than everyone else. Unfortunately that's not the answer you were looking for, so I'll be completely honest with you. About two years ago I had a dream that I was being hunted down. I died in that dream and woke up. After learning what it means to die in a dream I decided to fall back asleep and reenter that same dream. When I got back into the dream I was taught that with focus I could make anything that I wanted to happen, happen." He realized just how weird and cocky he had sounded all at once.

The boy expected a blank stare from Mr. Jensen, or some bullshit about how he should be checked out for psychiatric illness. Instead the answer given by the dimwitted teacher surprised the boy.

"What does it mean if you die in a dream Jake?"

"Umm." The boy was thrown off guard for moment. "Well according to most pre-colonialized cultures, death in a dream represents rebirth or a major life change. After reentering my dream I learned that through the power of focus I literally can do whatever the hell I want."

"Except homework?" Mr. Jenkins asked with a quirky smile.

"Except homework." Replied the boy. "It's menial labor. I learn better when I sit in front of something and try my own methods of deduction."

"Well said, Sherlock."

Mr. Jensen was starting to grow on the boy. The man was quicker than he seemed, and was keeping up with the boy's wit quite well. Not allowing the man to let his guard down, the boy inquired if he could leave now, as Mr. Jensen's mom was an impatient bitch.

"Oh trust me kid, I know. At least take her out to dinner for me. My new stepfather better be one hell of a gentleman," he joked.

"I'll make sure to do that sir." The boy replied.

"Good man" Mr. Jensen said, and as he turned back towards his desk the boy caught a glimpse of something in the man's eye. Maybe it was just a glint from the light, but he could've sworn he saw a touch of sincerity that hadn't been there previously.

"You have a good one Mr. Jensen, I'll see you tomorrow." The boy said as he turned back towards the door.

"I'll be here" replied the man as he sat back down in his squeaky swivel chair.

The boy threw his hood back on and made his way out of the classroom. The minute he was out of the building he sparked a cigarette and walked towards the parking lot. As he was nearing the gate to the parking lot he noticed a beautiful woman in tight black jeans and heels walking towards him.

"Hey kid! You know you aren't supposed to smoke on campus, right?" The woman said as he came closer.

"Fuck off lady, I'm on my way out." The usual response to get people out of his hair. The boy didn't care what people thought of him considering most people didn't think of him too highly.

"Good answer. Mind if I take a drag?"

Odd. As the boy approached the woman he stopped. She was certainly beautiful. Not in the stereotypical hot, high school girl way, but like how models on TV were beautiful. She had sharp edges to her face and defined cheekbones. She was skinny enough that super-tight jeans seemed loose on her. She held herself in a manner that made the boy wonder what she was doing asking a teenage weirdo for a bum of his stog. Another point of interest was the tattoo that ran from her shoulder down her left arm, forming a full sleeve. The monstrous head of the dragon started at her collarbone, and the snake-like body wormed its way down past her triceps, around her elbow, and ended at the inside of her wrist.

"Nice ink." the boy commented as she finally came to a stop in front of him.

"Thanks. Have any of your own?" She asked as she pulled the cigarette from the boy's fingertips.

"No my parents would kill me if I got any kind of tattoo."

It was true. As much as the boy had wanted to permanently mark up his body, he never had the balls to. He respected his parents too much. They had given him everything and anything he asked for and in return he had respected them enough to wait until he was living on his own.

"So you have the balls to tell a random lady to fuck off but you don't have the balls to go against your parents? Sounds like a load of crap to me."

"You don't know me. I happen to respect my parents more than anyone else."

"Good for you. Question though."

"Answer," the boy replied as he pulled the cigarette away from the woman and took a drag. He realized that he had started to walk with her towards the lunch tables. For someone intimidatingly good-looking, she was certainly magnetic.

"Have your parents ever disrespected you?" The woman inquired as she sat down on top of a table, resting her feet on the bench.

"Well no. I mean the only problems we ever have are when I come home late. Can't tell you how many nights I've come home and they pester me with stupid questions like where I was and who I was with."

"So they don't trust you?" she asked as she looked back at him with a smirk.

"I guess not. I never really gave them a reason to not trust me. They're just protective I suppose."

"So they don't trust you?" she asked again.

"No, they don't" the boy said as he began to think back on all the times he had come home completely sober and they made him walk in lines and say the alphabet backwards.

"Well that's a sign of disrespect. When you fire that same disrespect back at them the outcome is always entertaining."

"Oh really? Well I'll just head straight to the nearest tattoo shop then I guess."

"No need," The woman said. "I'm an artist out in LA. Come up with an idea and I'd be happy to draw it up for ya." As she said this she handed him a card. On the front was her name, number, and the logo of the shop she worked for. On the back were three pictures of tattoos, one of which was an intricately designed Buddha ripping a purple bong.

"Natalie Swanson." He read aloud. "You've got one hell of a pitch. Nice to meet you, I'm Jake Rivera" the boy said as he held out his hand.

"Pleased to meet you Jake." The woman took the boy's hand in her own and shook it.

"So what is a beautiful girl like you doing at a dump like this?" the boy asked.

"Wow look at you," She said as the cigarette was passed again. Her lips curled into a playful grin. "Telling me to fuck off and now calling me beautiful."

"Sorry about that. Most people aren't cool about cigarettes around here." The boy said, taking a drag.

"Well sorry bud, I'm actually here visiting my boyfriend."

"Ouch. The one-line shut down. Who's your boyfriend?"

"Alex."

"Last name?"

"Jensen."

"Wait. You mean Mr…" the boy was cut off by a voice to his right.

"Natalie, I see you've met Mr. Rivera."

The boy turned to see Mr. Jensen standing there, adjusting his Ray-Ban glasses in the light.

"Yeah, I was inviting him to the shop." The woman said as she stood and walked towards the teacher. As she got closer she reached her arms out to embrace the man.

"Mr. Rivera, I'll see you around. Enjoy your night." the teacher said.

"Have a good night sir." The boy replied as he stepped away from the table and began to walk towards the parking lot.

"See ya Jake." The woman said back as the boy started walking away.

"Later," the boy mumbled and continued walking.

As the boy placed the cigarette against his lips again he noticed just how empty the parking lot already was. How weird, he thought. Why are people so eager to leave school when all they do at home is the same shit? Most people got their homework done, ate, and watched TV or played video games for the rest of the night. What was so enticing about leaving? The boy concluded that the false idea of freedom at home was what motivated students to leave so quickly.

As the boy approached his car he was struck again by just how beautiful of a machine it was. Mr. Rivera—the boy's Father—was a semi-wealthy business owner of three separate hardware stores across Orange County. While the boy had never been spoiled, his father always rewarded him for hard work. His most recent accomplishment had been scoring a 2100 on the SAT. A ridiculous hustle on the boy's part. He let his Father believe that he had studied for weeks on end to get that score. When in reality he had only spent around fifteen minutes waiting for a guy to deliver him Adderall which he took the morning of the test. In return for scoring so high, his Father had rewarded the boy with a brand new 2017 Dodge Challenger. It was matte black with orange pinstripes, just like the poster that hung in the boys room.

After dumping his backpack in the trunk, the boy stepped into the custom racing seat made for the driver. Starting up the roaring engine, he threw the car in reverse and peeled out of the parking lot. Once he had hit the streets, he whipped a joint out of the center console and sparked it. Rolling his windows down at the stop light, he blew his smoke out and cranked the A/C up to full blast. With all the windows down and his air conditioner on the car was like a wind tunnel, no smell lingered by the time he pulled into the driveway. The boy stepped out of the car and shut the door. He then grabbed his backpack from the trunk before locking the car and heading up the pathway to his house.

Now that he had the familiar feeling of peace in the back of his mind, he casually opened the front door and made his way through the kitchen to his room. Upon passing by, the boy's Mom inquired how his day was.

"Good, boring." The boy replied like he always did. Just enough to keep her from questioning him further, but also not enough for her to wonder if something was wrong. Nothing was wrong, the boy thought as he closed the door to his room. It was just the same stupid shit day in and day out. Nothing new, nothing exciting.

The boy dropped his backpack on the floor and laid back into the bed, staring at the solid white stucco ceiling. He connected his phone to the speaker that sat on his nightstand and scrolled through the playlists until he found the one he was looking for. *The Police* began playing as his high mind wandered through the events of the day. "How weird," he thought as he reflected back to meeting Mr. Jensen's gorgeous girlfriend. How could such a sad life have such a great benefit? Why was Mr. Jensen such a burnout yet able to pull such a babe? The boy eventually concluded that some people's lives are a mystery. And unlike mystery novels or the shows on TV, the mysteries of other people's lives usually couldn't be solved. After deciding not to dwell on the subject, the boy resigned himself to lying in bed, listening to music, and enjoying his high.

He was awoken from a nightmare of dragons and 6-hour algebra lessons. A soft knocking at his door told him it was time for dinner. He slowly pulled himself out of bed and turned off the portable speaker on his nightstand.

"Alright I'm up Mom, I'll be out in a second," the boy grumbled.

"Okay hun, don't forget to wash up." His mom said as he heard her footsteps retreating back down the hall towards the kitchen.

The boy walked out the door and down to the bathroom. After using the toilet he stopped in front of the mirror. Eyedrops were a necessity as usual, so after blinking away tears he began to wash his hands. He thought about the stories that lived just below the skin of his hands. Blood from walls punched in frustration, sticky trichomes from rolling too much weed, tears wiped away as a kid trying to understand why everyone thought he was so weird.

His life had been a story, to say the least. A depressing one at that, but a story nonetheless. He imagined most teenagers probably thought the same about their lives.

Chapter 2

The boy grabbed a glass from the cupboard and began filling it with water. From the dining room he could hear his younger sister discussing the ins and outs of her day with her parents. Apparently, some guy had invited her to go ice skating and she was desperately asking her parents if she could go.

Maura was sixteen, tall, slender, beautiful, and smarter than shit. "Smarter than me" the boy thought as he sat down at the dinner table. The girl had made honor roll every year and was already getting letters from colleges like Berkeley, USC, and Georgia Tech. The boy liked to think he had taught his little sister everything she knew, but in all fairness she had picked most of it up on her own, much like the boy.

As much as the boy was the loner, stoner of their high school, his little sister was the polar opposite. She was head of her class, head cheerleader, and involved in everything from the debate club to "Hugs for the Homeless." His little sister was the epitome of everything he hated about high school, but the boy was so proud of her he was able to look past those things that disturbed him.

He sat down at the dinner table to a beautiful sight, his Mom had laid out mashed potatoes, melted-cheese broccoli, and tri-tip for dinner.

"Mom this looks awesome." The boy said gratefully.

"Well I had some help from the grocery store, but hey thanks anyways hun."

"Prayers." His Father said just as the boy was picking up his fork.

"Right." The boy grumbled as he took his sisters hand in one and his fathers in the other.

"Dear God, thank you for bringing us all home safely today." His father began.

"What's the point in saying prayers before a meal?" The boy wondered. He had never understood why you would pray before a meal. Why not after? It's not like blessing the food gave you superpowers or something, and who thanks the cook before they've tasted the meal? What if it's poisoned and it doesn't matter if we all got here safely?

Before the boy could finish his train of thought the prayer was over and he began to dig into the food. The tri-tip was phenomenal. The one thing that everybody said when they came over to the house was that his Mother could seriously cook. The boy knew his Mom was a great cook and considered himself lucky for having grown up with restaurant quality meals.

"So Jake, how was school today?" His father asked.

"Fine, just another day," the boy replied.

"Anything exciting happen?"

"No not really, I mean it's high school. Nothing exciting ever happens."

The boys father looked surprised.

"Really? No fights today? No druggies in the bathroom?"

The boy's Mother jumped in at this point. "Oh for God's sake Westley, not everyone went to a trashy high school like you!"

The Father seemed amused. "Oh and who else went to that trashy high school?" With a wink the father quickly stuffed his mouth and let out a hum of enjoyment to appease his wife and the look she was giving him. The boy was relieved, his Father had inadvertently taken the limelight away from himself and shut down the entire conversation, all in two sentences.

Most of the dinner continued with a satisfied silence. Occasionally conversation would pop up about a big band coming into town, or something the Father had seen while driving into work that day. Meaningless conversation to fill the awkward void of family dinners. This was how most dinners went, a constant peace-keeping.

After dinner the Father decided he would take over dish duty. After all, Mom had been working tirelessly over the meal and *American Idol* was on. The boy headed back to his room and after closing the door behind him he checked his phone. Three new text messages. The boy unlocked the phone and scrolled through the messages.

"Jake, hit me up when you read this. We're going out tonight."

"Jake where are you man???"

"Jake. Call me when you get this. We're tripping tonight."

"Why the fuck?" He muttered to himself.

The boy hadn't tripped before and had always been a little hesitant about hallucinogenic drugs. Even at a young age the boy had showed depressive tendencies. He had never considered himself depressed, or mentally unstable, but the idea of a bad trip frankly terrified the boy. All three messages were from Adam, so the boy figured why not see what the deal was. He had smoked with Adam several times before and trusted the other boy enough to give his proposition a chance.

"Never tripped before, what are we taking?" The boy replied.

"Acid." The one-word response came so fast the boy felt sure Adam had been waiting for his text.

Despite his own insecurities and fears about his ability to safely enjoy the drug, the boy had heard of good trips. He had also heard of some *really* good trips, where people came back more or less acting like they had found enlightenment. While these stories seemed like a stretch, it was enough of an incentive to give it a shot.

"Down. How much?" He sent back.

Agin, the reply was almost instant.

"Five dollar tabs. You should probably take one since it's your first trip. Lol"

"Alright well when and where am I meeting you?"

"I'll meet you at Ash Park in a half hour."

"Shit." The boy thought, "I guess I'm going out on a Wednesday." It was January, the coldest month in California, so the boy threw a coat on, grabbed his wallet, pack, and lighter, and turned to walk out the door of his bedroom.

"Hey Mom! I'm heading to Joe's, I'll be back later tonight!" The boy called down the hallway to his parents. He didn't expect to get off that easy, but he had his story made up already.

"Okay, what are you guys doing?" His mom inquired, standing up from the couch.

"We have a group project for physics, so we'll probably work on that for a little while then play Battlefield. Just hangin' out."

He'd used this cover countless times, always a different person, always a different class. Usually Battlefield was a constant.

"Alright well just let me know if you end up spending the night and tell Joe's Mom I said hi." His Mother responded with a smile as she sat back down.

"No drinking or injecting mari-ju-wana Jake." The boy's Father said with a chuckle.

"Of course Dad, only heroin. You know me." The boy replied sarcastically as he walked out the front door. He pulled the keys out from his pocket and slid into the Challenger. After plugging the aux cord into his phone he sent a quick text to Adam saying he was on his way.

As he pulled out of the driveway the boy thought about the relationship he had with his father. The boy had always gotten along well with the man. Obviously he didn't consider his father a friend, which the boy thought was good. He respected his Father more than he respected any friend. The man had put in work day in and day out to try and give the boy a relatively happy life.

"No friend would ever do that." The boy thought to himself. Yes, his father and he had a great relationship, with mutual respect. And then the words of Mr. Jensen's girlfriend kicked in. His Dad had always been strict when it came to the boys' social life. He had never been able to go to a party (on the rare occasion he actually asked), and when he would go out to smoke or hangout with a couple of the other kids from school his Dad would pester him as if he was coming back from a party. The boy then thought about tonight.

"If this trip lasts a while I might end up having to spend the night somewhere." The boy thought. And he damn sure wasn't going to spend the night with Adam. As much as he liked the other boy he knew for certain he was not gay or curious in any way, and felt like spending the night would only lead Adam on.

Then he thought about crashing in his car. The boy had done it before, plenty of times. It had always seemed sketchy though, and the racing seats weren't the most comfortable seats to sleep in. Nevertheless he knew it could be done, and if the trip came to that he was willing to just smoke some weed and pass out in the car.

He turned down the street that led to the park and lit up a cigarette. The boy was starting to feel excited. He had heard such great stories about acid. Stories about people finding themselves and their purpose in life. The more the boy thought about it the more he became enthralled by the idea. *What if he discovered his life's purpose tonight?*

The boy's excitement grew as he pulled into the parking lot. He first recognized Adam's white Scion, but the other, larger, Jeep wasn't familiar to the boy. The Jeep was on its way out so as the Challenger drew closer to it, the boy tried to glance inside at the driver. He couldn't make out even a vague silhouette though, as the Jeep was too high and moving too fast.

"Drug dealers." The boy said out loud in amusement. "Always so paranoid."

The boy pulled the challenger into a spot next to Adam's. After pulling the keys out of the ignition and locking the doors, he stepped out of the car, shooting Adam a head nod through the window as he did.

"What's up man?" The boy asked as he closed his door.

"Not much dude, just picked up two tabs for each of us," Adam replied with a grin.

"Two tabs?," the boy asked, feeling more than a little unnerved.

"Yeah you gotta take two your first time!," Adam exclaimed.

"You told me I should take one, since it was my first time." The boy snapped back.

"Well one tab if you want to take baby steps. If you take two tabs you'll get way better visuals, and besides this looks like really diluted acid. You'll only be doing like one and a half real tabs."

The boy thought for a moment. If he was going to discover his life's purpose, he would probably need to be tripping pretty hard.

The boy caved. "Alright, so I owe you ten then?"

"Yes sir. No stripper change please."

The boy glanced at his wallet. To be fair he did have enough one dollar bills to pay Adam back, but he didn't want to hear the flirtatious stripper jokes that would come along with doing so. The boy pulled out a ten and handed it to Adam.

"Thank you very much, and here are your two tabs," Adam said as he slid the bag into the boy's back pocket.

"Dude." The boy wasn't homophobic, but a move like that made him a little too uncomfortable.

"Oops, couldn't help myself. Anyways Jennifer should be here in a few minutes. She's trip-sitting us tonight."

The boy knew Jennifer Oslow. She was a pretty cool girl. One of the few girls smart enough to keep up with the boy's humor and sarcasm. Plus if she was trip-sitting he wouldn't have to deal with Adam playing games all night.

"Sounds good, so what's the plan?," the boy asked.

"Well we take these two tabs now, hangout here and wait for the trip to kick in. We can stay here for most of the trip because we can go check out the playground and spend some time in the park. If we need anything, Jennifer can drive us to wherever we need to go."

"Alright, well as long as she's fine with staying out all night that sounds fun," the boy replied as he pulled the bag out of his jeans. After opening it up and pulling out the folded tin foil inside, he unwrapped the two tabs. Two small, blue, paper rectangles with a white backing. Each edge had perforations on it, like the tabs had been torn apart.

"So I just put them on my tongue and let them sit?," the boy inquired. He knew the basics of dropping acid and didn't want to seem like a rookie to the more experienced tripper.

"Yep, if they don't dissolve within an hour or so you can go ahead and swallow them."

"Okay cool," the boy said as he placed each tab on his tongue. They didn't taste like anything, but felt like tiny tabs of paper, just how the boy had imagined them.

"It's going to feel kind of weird and they might move around a little bit on your tongue. Eventually they'll settle in though and you'll forget they're even in there," Adam said, noticing the face the boy was making.

"Ehkay, tho I'll be able to talk right?," the boy tried to spit out.

Adam doubled over in laughter, and the boy joined in after thinking about just how funny he sounded.

Adam put his two tabs in his mouth and replied, "yeth eggthacly." This brought tears to both of their eyes as they continued laughing. Once they had both composed themselves the boy pulled out another cigarette and lit it up, offering the pack to Adam. Instead of taking the pack the other boy pulled out his own.

"Newports, interesting choice," the boy stated, putting the little box back in his own pocket and taking a drag of the cigarette.

"Cheap and tasty," Adam replied.

The two boys leaned against their respective cars just as a third car rolled into the parking lot.

"That's Jfer," Adam stated after glancing up at the car. "I'd know that shitty Honda anywhere."

The shitty Honda in question looked to the boy like a 1998 Civic, with chromed out rims and a deteriorating paint job.

"Great, now we've got the sketchy car in the park at night. We're starting to look like legitimate degenerates," The boy observed.

"Hey, I happen to run a tight system here, I make sure degenerate is spelled loud and clear for those pigs who hardly know what it means," Adam joked back.

"Clearly," stated the boy as he looked Adam up and down. The other boy was wearing blue sneakers, dark jeans, and a black hoodie.

"You checking me out over there?," Adam asked with a grin.

"Jesus, Adam," The boy laughed it off, he enjoyed Adam's company. The other boy could certainly take a joke, and knew how to hand them out as well.

The two boys were interrupted by Jfer slamming her car door and strutting over to the two.

"What's up love?," Adam asked.

"My fucking Mom, I hate that woman!," Jfer exclaimed.

"Ohhh dear what is it this time. New boy toy?," Adam said as he took a drag of his cigarette.

"No just spends more time out than I do, and no matter how much I try to clean up after myself while she's gone the crazy bitch always comes home with an axe to grind." Jfer sighed and then looked up at the boy. "Hey Jake, can I bum a stoag off you?" The girl may have asked in a friendly enough way, but her look said "I need a cigarette. Now!"

"Sure, sorry to hear about your Mom. Sounds rough." The boy tried his best to act like he cared as he pulled out the pack and handed the girl a cigarette.

"It's fine, I just get worked up sometimes. Adam knows, he's usually the one I vent to," Jfer said as she smiled at Adam and lit her cigarette.

"Yeah I try to keep Jfer at least a little bit less crazy than her Mom. It's a burden of love." Adam smiled back at Jfer.

"So Jake, first trip?," inquired Jfer, trying to change the subject to their purpose for being out tonight.

"Yep," the boy replied as he stuck his tongue out to show Jfer.

"Two tabs, good choice. I took four my first time. Big mistake."

"Well yeah I can imagine! What was that like?," asked the boy.

"Okay so imagine acid opening a door in your mind, like a door to your third eye. So if you take one tab your first time, you can definitely crack that baby open. If you take two tabs, you'll get a sneak-peek at what's on the other side. Four tabs and that bitch gets blown off its hinges," Jfer said as the trio burst into laughter.

"Wow. Okay well I'm happy with two then," the boy muttered before taking a drag.

At this point Adam piped up "I wouldn't say that just yet. Wait until you get your sneak-peek behind that door. Jfer and I have both taken ten strips before. Now that was intense. Definitely not for the inexperienced tripper, but it was an experience that's for sure."

The boy looked at Adam in shock. Ten tabs? The boy was starting to wonder who these two crazies were. However, he realized that if he was going to trip with anybody for his first time, they would probably be his best guides.

"That sounds crazy. Did you know Hendrix used to put a ten strip in his headband before shows?," the boy said, trying to flex a little of his drug knowledge. He had read it while doing a paper on Hendrix for Rock History.

"Yeah I believe it," Jfer started "Acid can be absorbed into any pore on your body, so if he was up on stage sweating he was probably tripping pretty hard."

"How crazy would that be?," Adam asked rhetorically. "Like, can you imagine being on stage in front of all those people and you're trippin nuts?"

"Well that's probably why his concerts were so crazy. Have you ever seen old footage of him on stage? The dude was practically levitating." The boy stated.

"Alright guys, well can we please smoke?," Jfer asked. "Since I'm not tripping I'd at least like to be high so I can enjoy watching you two."

"Yeah, my car or yours?," Asked Adam.

The boy jumped in. "We can smoke in mine, I keep my bong in my back seat."

"Look at Jake coming in clutch with the bong," said Adam as he nodded in approval. "How's about you grab the bong and we smoke in my car, it's probably a little roomier than yours."

The boy took a look at Adam's box-like scion. It would definitely be more comfortable than squeezing into the challenger, so he agreed and went around to open the door to his car. Reaching into the back seat with one hand the boy set his keys in the cupholder and used the other hand to balance himself against the steering wheel. Once he had grabbed the bong he locked the door and closed it, bringing the black padded sleeve out into the view of the other two.

"And he's got a sleeve for it and everything," said Jfer, obviously impressed as she shot a look in Adam's direction.

"I'm a bit of a glass connoisseur," replied the boy, taking pride in the first bong he had ever bought. He hadn't been smoking long, but the boy had jumped headfirst into stoner culture.

The three jumped into Adam's car, Jfer let the boy take shotgun so he could look out the front window once he started tripping. This made the him realize just how long ago he had taken the acid. He and Adam had first placed the tabs on their tongues about a half hour earlier, which meant he was nearing the start of his trip.

Once they had gotten situated the boy pulled the sleeve off his prized possession, Revealing a fourteen inch, double honey comb masterpiece. It was a three hundred dollar piece, but the ice catcher had a chip in it so the boy was able to work the price down to two hundred.

"Damn son, where'd you find that?," asked Jfer with obvious admiration.

"The little smoke shop just off of Chafey Street, they hooked it up for a discount because we're homies," the boy bragged. He knew the car was dark and the two would never notice the small chip in the ice catcher.

"Nice, how long have you been smoking? I honestly didn't even know you did anything until Adam told me I was trip sitting you two."

"I've been smoking off and on for about a year now. Started smoking every day about three months ago. That was when I got the bong actually, I wanted a really nice piece to show off," the boy said with a smile.

Jfer obviously approved as she gave a quick laugh and plucked the bowl from the bong. "So should we just match?," she asked as she pulled out her own medicinal marijuana container.

"I'm dry right now," Adam said with a sad look on his face.

"Bastard. Wait don't you sell weed?" Jfer exclaimed, clearly a little irritated that Adam had brought her out on a school night and couldn't even smoke her out.

"Nah, I had to get out. I started catching heat at the school. Mr Jensen came in clutch for me at one point but even he told me to slow it down."

The boy was astounded. Mr. Jensen? The same Mr. Jensen that had until today been a boring, unsophisticated pratt? Before he could even begin to form a question about this new revelation, Jfer spoke in a cool and collected tone. As if Mr. Jensen being involved with drugs on campus was no big deal.

"That sucks. How did Jensen come in clutch this time?," Jfer asked as she pulled a single, half gram nug out of her bottle and placed it in the open grinder on her lap.

"I got pulled into the Principal's Office because he had been alerted that I was in possession of drugs on campus. Luckily I was hanging out in Mr. Jensen's room at lunch when the call went out on the intercom. He told me I should leave my backpack in his room because he had heard some of the teachers talking about me before school. So I dropped the backpack in his room and only brought my iPad in its case up to the office. The principal asked to search my backpack, I told him all I brought to school that day was my iPad. He went through my case and sent me back to lunch with a stern warning."

The boy was in shock. But then again after the events of today he could see Mr. Jensen as being "that chill teacher who looks out for his students.," The boy had always loved teachers like that, especially since they usually didn't tolerate ass-kissing.

"Damn, Mr. Jensen is a boss!," The boy stated with wide-eyed excitement, "I had no idea he was that chill."

Jfer looked at the boy like he was completely out of the loop. "Oh yeah dude, you didn't know? Mr. Jensen has saved so many kids asses before. I heard last year he taped some girl's bag of Xanax under his desk so she wouldn't get caught by a drug dog."

"Yeah man, Mr. Jensen is the homie. I could've sworn the O in my bag looked a little smaller when I got back though." Adam said with a look in his eyes, pondering what had happened. "I wouldn't be surprised if the guy stole a couple grams from me. Shit I'd give him a couple of grams for warning me like that."

"Okay Adam. I think you were just a little paranoid about your product," Jfer said with a smirk as she cracked open the grinder.

"Jfer what strain is that?," inquired the boy, still half in shock about the recent revelation, and half inquisitive about the sweet, skunky smell that was filling the car.

"It's this crazy new one called Death Star. The Red Room just got this stuff a couple days ago from a new grower. It's nuts, do you like indicas?"

"Well it smells really good, and being couchlocked is the type of high I really enjoy, so throw that in the bowl!," The boy replied.

"Well that's perfect, because this stuff will make your trip that much more relaxing." Jfer said with a smile. "Here. Your bong, your greens," she said before setting the bowl piece back in it's stem.

"What a doll, thanks Jfer," the boy said as he pulled a lighter out of his pocket. He glanced down at his phone and realized he had taken the tabs almost forty five minutes ago. He figured if the acid wasn't taking effect by the end of the bowl he would swallow the tabs. Just as the boy put his lips to the glass and flicked the lighter he noticed something. The small flame seemed different. Like a small glimmer of light in the middle of the dark car, and every detail of the green bowl seemed to stick out to him.

The boy lit just a corner of the bowl and pulled in air until the entire bong was white-walled. "Why not show off one more time?"

The boy thought. After pulling the bowl up from the bong he cleared the entire thing, sucked in what little oxygen his lungs could still hold, and leaned his head back. After a couple seconds the boy exhaled, then opened his eyes to view a whole new world.

Chapter 3

"Jake. Jake you good?," Adam was looking at the boy with concern.

"Dude. I am great. I think I'm trippin," the boy replied. "Marco!"

"Polo!," shouted Jfer as she reached for the bong.

Adam used a curse word of choice and looked over at the boy. "So what do you see man?"

"Okay well for starters, there are small rainbows around every light in the park right now. And then the leaves on the trees just look really, I don't know, high def," the boy said as he continued staring out the window in awe.

"Yep, he's definitely trippin," said Jfer with a laugh. She then proceeded to rip the bong as hard as the Buddha did in the tattoo on Natalie's card. Instantly Jfer broke out into a fit of coughing, and had to take a sip of her water. "Jake. That bong is a beast, my friend," the girl squeezed out between coughs.

The boy laughed at this, he was happy that he had impressed Jfer. While people's opinions of him generally didn't matter to the boy, he liked the girl. And despite the fact that the only two people he had smoked with were Adam and his hippie neighbor, he identified the girl as someone he would want to smoke with sometime.

"Thanks, I call him Mushu," the boy said with a proud smile.

"Mushu!," the girl exclaimed with a huge smile. "Like the little dragon from Mulan?"

"Yep, it's not the biggest bong, but it packs a punch like Mushu."

"That's great. I love it," Jfer said as she handed Adam the bong.

Adam turned to grab the glass and sarcastically joked "look at you two, flirting over a bong."

"Oh shut up Adam. I just learned like fifteen minutes ago that Jake was a stoner. I'm allowed to be excited," Jfer shot back. But as soon as Adam turned she looked at the boy and gave him a look that seemed to say "he's not lying."

The boy smiled back and made an attempt to wink at Jfer. The boy had never been good at winking so it ended up looking more like a twitch than anything else. Luckily the girl had a sense of humor as she began giggling and imitating the boy with a weird twitch of her own eye.

"Okay, so she's definitely flirting with me," thought the boy. He turned to see Adam staring at the two of them. With a shake of his head the other boy pressed his lips to the glass and took a hit. Adam's hit far surpassed either of the other two's. And after he held it in for longer than either of them he slowly exhaled and filled the car with smoke. Or maybe he didn't fill the car with smoke. It seemed like smoke was pouring out of Adam like a chimney. The boy suddenly remembered that he was tripping, and felt a wave of relief hit him. "If this is the acid affecting me then I should be fine. It's not bad at all. Pretty cool actually," the boy thought.

The bong was once again passed to the boy and he flicked the lighter to reveal an empty bowl.

"Adam! You son of a bitch you cleared the bowl!," the boy exclaimed.

"What? No man that was Jfer! I just pulled it through!"

"Bullshit!," retorted Jfer, "You're tripping dude. I watched you torch the entire thing and then pull it through!"

"Oh. Well damn maybe I did," Adam said with apprehension.

"It's cool, I'll just load the next one," the boy replied as he pulled out his own green pill bottle. "Jfer have you ever smoked Sour D?" He asked.

"One of my all-time faves," she replied with a wink and a mischievous smile. Not a twitch, but a wink.

"Love Sour D," Adam murmured. Both Jfer and the boy looked at Adam at the same time. He had one hand on the keys which were in the ignition, and one hand on the steering wheel. Meanwhile his eyes were locked on the streetlight just in front of the car.

"Adam you better not be trying to drive," Jfer warned.

"Oh shit, what? No, no I was just going to turn the key halfway so we could listen to music."

"Good. I didn't think you were that stupid," the girl replied.

"So wait, what happens if you try to drive while tripping?," the boy asked.

"Well, I've never done it, but I mean imagine trying to drive when the lane markers start turning into floating noodles," Adam explained.

"No bueno," said Jfer. "You know Austin Ellis right?"

The boy knew who Austin Ellis was, he had worked with the stocky wrestler on a group project before. He usually gave the boy a nod or a "what's up man" when they passed each other on campus. "Yeah, I know his face," the boy responded.

"Well he was tripping last December and got in a huge crash," Jfer continued. "Slammed into a tree. Miraculously he didn't get a single scratch on him, but it just goes to show. Don't trip and drive." As Jfer said this she handed the boy her grinder.

"That's crazy. Yeah I'll make sure not…" the boy was cut off by a boy band blasting through the speakers.

"FUCK ADAM TURN IT DOWN!" Shrieked Jfer.

Adam quickly reached for the dial and cranked it down to a more tolerable level.

"Sorry guys, I like to jam out sometimes," Adam said with a nervous smile.

"To that shit?," the boy asked with a look of disdain on his face. '

"You stupid, stupid, idiot," Jfer said as she hit Adam with the bong sleeve between each insult.

This led to Adam complaining about homophobia and hate crime while Jfer laughed and hit him with the sleeve a couple more times. While all of this was going on the boy couldn't help but become entranced by the weed he had ground up. He didn't remember pulling a nug out of the bottle, or even having his grinder in his pocket. But there he was, sitting with a bong between his legs and ground up weed in his hand.

"Whoah. Guys I'm buggin hard right now," the boy said with a chuckle. The chuckle grew into a laugh, and all of a sudden he was laughing. Not the kind of laughter that causes people to think you're crazy, or weird. The kind of laugh that naturally makes everyone around you join in. All three of the car's occupants were laughing hysterically when finally Adam asked what the boy was tripping over.

"I don't know. Like I know I pulled my own weed out of my pocket, but I don't remember pulling out my grinder, or dropping a nug into it."

"Dude. That's my grinder. You don't remember doing all of that because I literally just put the grinder in your hand to pack a bowl," Jfer said before continuing her laughter.

"Oh what?" The boy asked incredulously. He knew he was tripping now, and so did Jfer and Adam apparently because they were sharing a look that unnerved the boy. Almost as if they knew something that he didn't.

"What's up with the look?," the boy asked as the two broke into smiles simultaneously.

Adam looked back at the boy. "Nothing, we just love watching people trip for their first time. You're going to be fun to trip with, I can tell," he said with a smirk.

"What makes someone fun to trip with?," the boy inquired.

It was Jfer who answered this time. "Well if they're funny or you know they're enjoying their trip it just makes it better for everyone else. It makes it easier for other people to enjoy their trip."

"Hm. Okay cool. Well feel free to laugh your ass off, I'm enjoying myself." This time the boy let off a grin of his own, and began packing the next bowl.

The second bowl went around in the same rotation, and since Adam was careful not to torch it this time, it made two rounds through the trio before the boy had to dump it.

"Okay. Time for a stoag," declared Adam.

"Yes! Thank you!" Exclaimed Jfer.

As the group opened the doors smoke billowed out of the car like the windows in a house fire.

"Jake, dude. Look up at the street light," Adam said in awe as he stretched his legs.

As he did so, the boy was hit with the sight of smoke moving across the glow emanating from the light. He had never seen anything like it. The smoke seemed to be effecting the light so that shafts of orange were streaming from the dim bulb.

"That's incredible," the boy said with a smile. He could stare at the sight for hours it seemed, but he had to break away and look at something else. He didn't want to start tripping too hard this early in the night.

"Alright, Jake come here," said Jfer.

"Why what's up?," the boy asked as he turned towards the girl.

"Hold out your hand."

So the boy did, his fingers seemed different. Longer, more elegant.

"No idiot make a fist," the girl said with a laugh.

The boy closed his fingers and watched as Jfer slipped a rubber band around his wrist.

"What's this for?," the boy asked as he looked up inquisitively.

"In case you start tripping too hard or for too long, just snap that thing against your wrist and it'll bring you back to reality."

"Oh, thanks," the boy said. He knew he had chosen the right people to trip with. These two obviously knew what they were doing, and were going to watch over him.

"No problem. Now give me a cigarette I'm fiending," Jfer replied with a smirk.

The boy let out a chuckle and pulled the pack out of his pocket. Handing one to the girl and putting one between his own lips he lit the cigarette. Again the little flame seemed so intriguing. The way it swayed with the slight breeze. As he pulled on the end of the cigarette to get it lit he let out small puffs of smoke on either side of his mouth. The small clouds began to twist and worm their way through the night air. The boy loved what he was seeing. It was almost as if all of the little things he had never noticed in everyday life were suddenly beautiful sights and sounds. The breeze blowing through the trees sounded like waves crashing on a beach. The sizzling sound of the tobacco and chemicals in his cigarette was a frying pan sautéing some sort of food. The small trail of smoke on the end of his stoag was a swirling and twirling grey contrail, being pulled up into the night.

After taking in his surroundings for a minute the boy returned his attention to the girl standing in front of him.

"Beautiful isn't it?," she asked.

"Yeah, I mean I get what you mean by seeing things through your third eye," the boy said back, still in awe of everything going on around him.

"Trust me hon you haven't seen anything yet. Give it another hour or two and you'll be on a whole different level."

"So how long do you think I'll be tripping?," the boy asked to no one in particular.

"Well it's nine-thirty right now, so with two tabs you'll be coming down around three, sober by five," Adam stated matter-of-factly.

"Five in the morning?," the boy asked rhetorically. "Well I suppose I better tell my mom I'm spending the night."

"Yeah that's probably a good idea. Oh and I hope you don't plan on sleeping afterwards either. You probably won't be able to sleep until you get home from school tomorrow."

"Why?," the boy asked out of pure interest.

This time it was Jfer that answered. "Well acid causes your brain to fire neurons way faster than normal, so it takes a while after you're done tripping for your brain to slow itself down. Or at least that's my theory. We've never really looked into it to be honest."

"Interesting," the boy said, pondering the aspects of the brain and how the chemicals in acid would effect it. He didn't want to think too hard about it, considering he was sure it wasn't a good affect. He decided to try out the rubber band to see if it would work. He snapped himself on the wrist and instantaneously snapped out of the negative thought process.

"Works huh?," Jfer said smugly.

"Yeah that literally snapped me right out of it," the boy replied.

"Hey look at you with the puns," Adam said as he quietly laughed and took a drag of his cigarette.

The boy was reminded of his own cigarette and after flicking the ash off of the end he put the little death stick up to his lips. As he inhaled the warm and familiar smoke into his lungs, he turned towards the park, and saw the playground in the distance gleaming under the moonlight. Suddenly the boy looked up and realized why tonight of all nights, he was tripping.

"Adam. You planned this night didn't you?" The boy asked, happily looking up at the bright, white, full moon. It was almost like a spotlight, one that covered the entire park. The lampposts and street lights didn't really seem necessary as the boy began to notice just how bright the park was. He could see everything from a leftover tee-ball tee to the growing dew on the grass just yards ahead of him, glimmering in the moonlight.

"What, you mean the full moon? Honestly I didn't, but that's a good omen as far as I'm concerned," the other boy said as he too began to look up at the spotlight that radiated through the darkness, opening up the night to what seemed like endless possibilities.

"So boys, shall we loiter in the park?," Jfer said as she walked past the two.

Suddenly it dawned on the boy that this park was not just for looking at. It was a physical place. This mystical land that seemed to be glowing under the light of the moon was just a mere feet in front of him, waiting for his exploration!

"Definitely," the boy said as he stepped out of the streetlight and into the silvery light of the moon.

Chapter 4

The park was like something out of a dream the boy thought as his feet made swishing sounds over the dew-laden grass. Under the illumination of the full moon the entire field seemed to be a growing, glowing, alien landscape. The boy stared out at the far end of the field, which seemed to be growing farther and farther away with every second that passed. Finally Adam broke the serene silence.

"So, what do you think Jake?"

"It's amazing. I feel like we're walking on the moon or something," the boy said with wonder and awe in his eyes.

"Yep, it's a pretty eye-opening experience," Adam replied back.

The trio continued walking in silence as both boys took stock of their surroundings. How could the boy have ever been worried about acid? This was unlike anything he had ever seen before. He was keeping a tight grip on the trip, trying not to let it slip out of his grasp. But after a minute or so of walking in silence the boy decided to let his mind wander, to let it explore all the new possibilities and doorways that it had been opened to.

As he looked at the trees across the field he saw patterns in the gentle swaying of the leaves, patterns unlike anything he had seen before. The boy was transfixed as his mind began to focus harder on the patterns. This made them stand out even more, almost as if the patterns were moving from the trees out across the field towards him. With a snap of the rubber band the boy broke his concentration and came back to reality. Or something closer to reality.

The trio was almost at the playground, and as the boy was about to step into the sandbox he was stopped by a voice behind him.

"Make sure you take your shoes and socks off," said Jfer as she crouched down to untie her Converse.

So the boy did, and as he was pulling his foot from the shoe he saw the patterns again in the grass at his feet. They weren't overbearing, or making him nervous, they were just there. Almost like the white foam that sits on top of ocean water, the patterns were sitting on top of the grass. Finally the boy had his shoes and socks off so he stood back up with both in hand and took his first step into the sand.

His first thought was about how cold the sand was. The temperature had gotten down to around sixty degrees. With the dewfall, the top of the sand had become cold and moist. As the boy's foot sunk deeper into the sand he noticed an almost massaging feeling on his foot. The deeper his foot sank into the sand the warmer it became. It had been a clear and sunny day so the sand had sat and absorbed the warmth of the sunlight for hours. This caused the dramatic change in temperature between the top level of sand and the level three inches deeper.

"It's like walking on a marshmallow with a warm interior," the boy said, then realizing how ridiculous he sounded he began laughing. This prompted all three of them to laugh before Jfer replied.

"Well yeah I mean I guess that's one way to look at it. I call it sand but hey whatever works for you." Jfer let out another short laugh and led the way up to the playground.

Adam was following behind her and the boy brought up the back, intrigued by the strange sensation the sand had on his feet. As the trio arrived at the gazebo Jfer made her way up the child-sized ladder and stepped onto the platform. While Adam made his way up the ladder the boy began to dig his feet deeper into the sand. Finally when it was his turn to climb up the ladder the boy looked up with happiness in his eyes.

"Can I just stay and play in the sand?," he asked giddily.

This brought more laughter to the group and Jfer responded "Jake come up here you can play in the sand in a minute just come look at this first."

So the boy sighed and made his way up the ladder, the cold metal stinging the bottom of his feet. Once he had reached the top he straightened up and looked out over the sandbox.

"Oh my God," was all the boy could get out.

"Pretty cool right?" Adam said as he gazed out at the same strange landscape the boy was seeing.

From an elevated viewpoint, the footprints left behind in the sand by children throughout the day traced patterns across the originally blank slate. It reminded the boy of craters on the moon, and as he stared across the vast expanse the craters seemed to move almost eratically. The boy was stunned.

"Some people want to travel the world to see different landscapes," started Jfer, "I prefer to take drugs and watch as familiar and every-day landscapes change around me."

"Spoken like a true burnout," Adam said with a smirk.

"I've always wanted to travel," said the boy. "But something tells me I won't see this anywhere else in the world. It's like a totally different world"

Just as the boy was saying this he felt arms wrap around his waist from behind. Jfer broke the awkward silence by whispering "What do you see Rose?," in the boy's ear.

"Titanic. Nice reference," the boy said. "I see craters, all the footsteps in the sand look like craters on the moon."

"Well aren't you two cute," Adam stated with sarcasm dripping.

The boy turned to face Jfer. He hadn't really noticed it before, but the girl was beautiful in the silvery glow of the moonlight. Her dark brown hair contrasted with her glistening green eyes. The boy was entranced.

"Is there something on my face?," the girl asked in amusement.

"Yeah there's a purple turtle crawling across your nose right now," the boy said back jokingly.

This prompted laughter from all three of them, and the boy who had never asked for friends, never saw the use for them in the first place, inadvertently knew he had gained two new friends.

Chapter 5

The trip continued on in such a fashion that the boy was comfortable and enjoying himself. Everything had new meaning to him, and he looked at all of his surroundings in a new light. Everything from playing in the sandbox to walking through the ivy bushes that surrounded the residential wall of the park. The slide was the boy's favorite part though. As he stepped into the dark entrance of the slide he felt like he was stepping into a black hole. Then as he propelled himself downward his vision would go black until he fell out at the bottom. Face-up, staring at the black starry night the boy would watch as the stars danced in front of him.

He would then sit up and turn his gaze to the trees in front of him. Watching the leaves was almost melodic. As he looked around and became more aware of his surroundings he'd stand, and run back to meet with Jfer and Adam. The night was truly an adventure. After a couple hours the boys' trips were peaking so the group walked out into the grass and laid back, looking up at the stars.

"What a crazy view," the boy stated after a couple seconds.

"You know there's only like six stars out right?" Said Jfer.

"Yeah but they look like a galaxy or something." Adam said, backing the boys' statement. "Besides, orion's Belt is out and that's the cool one."

"God you two are tripping nuts right now," Jfer replied with a smile showing she enjoyed watching the boys.

Then the group sat in silence for a while. Nobody spoke Jfer was enjoying her high while the boys tripped out over a galaxy of six stars. As the boy looked up at the stars he decided now was the best time to discover his true life meaning. He knew acid made this possible, and after all, he had taken two tabs. Why not try and uncover some hidden meaning to life?

The first question the boy asked himself was "What am I good at?" The boy was an avid movie watcher and enjoyed reading, but somehow he knew that directing wasn't within his reach. He then considered acting or being a movie critic. As he thought about these options he came to the conclusion that he wasn't much of an actor and being a critic would involve writing anyways.

All of these options presented him as a storyteller in some form or another, so the boy decided that's where he must be heading. Possibly photography? Maybe cinematography? either way he went he'd be able to share a story based off of his own perspective with other people. The boy imagined that was the ultimate answer he was seeking. he would be a storyteller, in some fashion or another.

The boy's train of thought was cut off by Adam slowly pushing himself up off the grass. The boy turned to face Adam and inquire where he was going, but Jfer had turned her head in the opposite direction. She had a funny look on her face, like she was trying to figure out a puzzle, or decipher a code of some kind.

"He likes to walk around when he's tripping. Can't stay in one place for more than a couple minutes," Jfer said quietly.

"Shouldn't we go with him in case he wanders off?" The boy questioned nervously.

"Nah he never makes it outside the park. He sometimes walks around it under the glow of the streetlamps," the girl said.

The boy must have looked concerned still because Jfer added "He always finds his way back though like a lost puppy."

"How cute." The boy replied somewhat sarcastically.

"Want to go wait for him on the playground?" The girl inquired after a moment of silence.

"Sure." The boy responded as he pushed himself up into a sitting position and slowly stood up. He felt a slap on his ass as he did so the boy looked back at Jfer with incredulity.

"Bitch, you gotta pay for this ass," the boy said with false attitude as he stuck his hand out to the girl.

"Oh, shut up!" Jfer exclaimed before giggling and taking the boys hand.

The boy pulled the girl to her feet and realized they were standing very close now. The two locked eyes and shared a moment.

"What was that?" The boy asked.

"I don't know. You tell me," the girl replied with a grin.

"I don't know. I guess we'll have to find out," the boy replied, returning the smile.

"I suppose," Jfer said as she stood on her tiptoes and kissed the boy.

As soon as it had begun, it was over. The boy wasn't sure if they had kissed for minutes or a second. Time was incoherent because of the trip. All he knew was that Jfer was walking away in the direction of the playground.

As the boy looked in the distance, the playground seemed miles away. He caught up to Jfer and mentioned this to her. She advised him to keep watching the playground as they walked. The boy did so, and as they moved closer the playground seemed to be moving farther and farther away until they had finally reached the sandbox.

"Wait. How did we get here? The playground looked like it was miles away." The boy said, not comprehending how he had managed to travel so quickly to a destination that had seemed moments earlier to be fading into the distance.

"Crazy, right?" The girl replied. "It's the best when you're walking down a hallway and it seems so long until you somehow find yourself at the end."

"How does that happen?" The boy asked excitedly, as if the girl had all the answers he needed.

"I honestly have no idea. They're called drugs for a reason dude," Jfer said with a laugh.

"Oh well excuse me. First time tripper here," the boy shot back.

"Well I must say Jake, you've been holding it together pretty well. How many times have you had to use that rubber band tonight?" She asked, looking down at the boy's wrist.

"I've been using it about every five minutes," the boy said as he looked at the girl and smiled. "Thanks for it by the way, and thanks for trip-sitting."

"Of course." The girl replied. "Always fun to watch people for their first time."

"Can I offer you a cigarette in return?" The boy asked.

"Jake Rivera you're an angel," stated Jfer as she leaned in and kissed the boy again.

She led him up the ladder onto the top level of the gazebo and the boy wrapped his arm around her waist as they sat back against a red plastic wall. The boy dug the pack out of his pocket and pulled two cigarettes out, offering one to Jfer and putting one to his own lips.

"Pretty girls don't light their own cigarettes," the boy stated as he set his small flame to the end of the girl's stoag.

"Thanks ugly," The girl replied playfully.

The boy then lit his own cigarette and slipped both the pack and the lighter back into his pocket.

The two sat in silence before Jfer finally popped a question.

"So why have I never seen you at one of Adam's parties?" She asked, looking at the boy.

"I don't know. I guess I never really wanted to be a part of the whole 'party crowd'. I always thought most of them were stuck-up and kind of annoying," the boy replied, being brutally honest with the girl.

"So do you think I'm stuck-up and annoying?"

"No, not you, not Adam either. I just feel like based off of how a lot of those kids act at school that's how they'd be outside of school too, you know?"

"I think you should give them a chance. Most people are nothing like how you would expect based off of school. Take me and Adam for example, we're both pretty reserved people at school but Adam throws some of the biggest parties and I'm a huge stoner."

"True, you are a huge stoner," the boy said as he poked the girl in the ribs.

"Oh shut up." She said with a giggle. "Hey speaking of which we should go grab Adam and smoke another bowl."

"Good idea, where'd he wander off to?" The boy asked as he stood up, overlooking the park.

Adam was lying down on a bench with an unlit cigarette in his mouth and his hoodie balled up under his head acting as a makeshift pillow. The rainbows around the lights were beginning to grow less intense. But then again, everything in the boy's peripheral vision was squirming and twisting into dizzying patterns and colors. The sandbox now looked to the boy like an aerial shot of the ocean. Each footprint the crest of a wave.

"Yo! Adam!" Jfer called out.

He sat up and waved at the two. "How was he?" Adam directed at Jfer.

She blushed and asked Adam to kindly fuck off, then informed him of the decision to smoke more.

"Sounds good, let's go," Adam replied, lighting the cigarette that had been sitting on his lips.

The walk back to the car wasn't too bad. The boy kept his eyes on the grass in front of him or the two people beside him most of the way. As fun as it was, he didn't feel like tripping over the distance to the car. Besides, he was entertained by the conversation between Jfer and Adam.

"All I'm saying is that salvia is way better than shrooms." Adam was arguing.

"Dude last time you made me do salvia with you I thought I was lost at sea." Jfer countered.

"But you were swimming in my carpet! You were fine!"

"It doesn't matter, I never enjoy my trip when I smoke Salvia. Shrooms always gives me a euphoric hippy-trip."

"Jake have you tried salvia or shrooms?" Adam asked, trying to get a third-party opinion.

"Nope, this is the first time I've ever tripped, like on anything," the boy replied sheepishly.

"Really?" Jfer asked rhetorically. "Most people start with shrooms considering they're a little easier to handle."

"Adam, I told you it was my first time tripping earlier when we were texting," the boy said bemusedly. He was surprised that Adam had forgotten such a crucial detail of the night so easily.

"Oh, I thought you meant tripping acid! My bad," Adam said apologetically. "Well you're handling two tabs really well then!" He added. Offering his knuckles out for the boy to pound.

"Yeah thanks, I'm just trying to take it all in. It's a lot to handle but I'm definitely enjoying it." The boy replied as he tapped his knuckles against Adam's.

The boy took one last drag of his cigarette before flicking the butt into the parking lot. As the group came closer to the Scion Adam pulled the keys out of his pocket and hit the unlock button. The car gave two short responses of the horn and the doors could be heard unlocking.

The boy offered Jfer passenger seat but she politely declined again, saying she could stretch out in the back seat so he could enjoy staring out the window like before. The boy took shotgun again and pulled the bong off the floor, placing it in his lap.

"Jfer can you please hand me a water bottle?" Adam asked back to the girl.

"Me too please," the boy added.

"Nope," Jfer replied as she reached under the driver seat and pulled out three water bottles, handing two of them to the boys in front and setting one on the seat beside her.

"Want me to pack the bowls this time?" Jfer asked, reaching into the center console to pull out her grinder.

"Yeah but we can smoke my weed if you want." The boy replied.

"Okay cool. So Adam how does it feel to be bumming weed off of people?" Jfer poked.

"Feels great. Free weed is the best weed," He fired back jokingly.

The boy reached back into his pocket and pulled out the small green nug-jug which contained his "medicinal" marijuana. As he handed a nug back to Jfer he asked what symptoms she gave the doctor in order to get her card.

"I fed him the insomnia line. Which is actually true, I can't sleep unless I take like two or three bowls to the face." She responded.

"Adam do you have your card?" The boy inquired.

"You mean a medcard?" Adam asked, breaking his blank stare into the distance.. "No I've always just picked up from other people, and back when I was dealing it was so much cheaper to get it from the private growers than from a clinic. Plus I could buy in bulk that way."

"Makes sense." The boy replied as he began to trip on the condensation building around the windows. The thin layer of water lay on the glass like a thin silken sheet. Allowing the boy to see through it, but causing his vision of the outside world to be blurred.

"Is it cool if I get greens?" Asked Jfer, breaking the boy's concentration.

"Yeah of course, you packed it you smoke it," The boy said. Immediately followed by "deuces!"

"SON OF A BITCH!" Exclaimed Adam in frustration. "I thought we were playing Marco Polo again!"

"Sorry bud, gotta be quick on your toes." The boy said with a smirk.

He then turned to watch Jfer take a good-sized rip before slowly exhaling a plume of smoke.

"How did I forget about the sunroof?" Adam asked as he slid the cover back, allowing a bright silver shaft of light to come streaming into the car, penetrating the darkness that had been there only seconds ago.

Jfer passed the bong up to the boy who thanked her and placed it in his lap. After lighting the corner of the bowl he managed to take a substantial hit. The boy held his smoke for a couple seconds before slowly exhaling through his nose and the sides of his mouth. He watched as the smoke trailed down and out of his nose before ascending back up into the shaft of moonlight. He thought about how he must have looked while doing the smoke trick and understood why people called it "the dragon."

The boy passed the bong to Adam, and sunk back into his seat, moving his gaze out across the park. Once again he started to trip over just how eerily beautiful the park looked under the full moon. Almost like a horror movie without the terrifying monster chasing people.

"SNICK!" The boy snapped the rubber band against his wrist. Anxiety had crept in the moment he began thinking about a horror movie. "I have to be careful," the boy thought, "I still have plenty of time for this trip to go wrong, can't screw it up now that I've enjoyed it so much already."

Smoking definitely reinforced the acid, so that even once the boy's trip had started to slow down, he was still noticing the patterns and beauty in things when he stopped to focus on them long enough.

The bong was passed around once more before Jfer declared the bowl to be cashed. Prompting the question of whether to load another bowl or go get food. After much debate the trio decided to make one more excursion into the park, come back to the car, smoke, and then visit a twenty-four hour taco shop nearby.

The second excursion into the park was mostly uneventful. Adam played in the sand while the boy and Jfer watched. The two would sit atop their throne of a gazebo and talk or laugh between drags of their cigarettes.

Jfer ended the stay at the park after about an hour, and led the group back towards the cars.

By the end of the fourth bowl the boy was convinced that he was now tripping harder than he had at any other part of the night. His peripheral vision was clouded with spinning shapes and flashing colors, while if he let his gaze land on anything for too long it would start to unravel in front of him. What he used to see as a park bench suddenly became a model of Stonehenge.

The boy resigned himself to sitting back and relaxing while he embraced the trip. Soon Jfer switched seats with Adam and the three were off on another adventure to find cheap and greasy Mexican food.

Chapter 6

As Jfer pulled out of the parking lot and began to pick up speed down the quiet and empty street the boy couldn't help but to stare in wonder out the window. As soon as he recognized an object in his field of view, they were already flying past it.

"It feels like I'm in a spaceship moving at the speed of light." The boy said with a laugh.

"If you think this is cool wait until we get to the stop light," Jfer replied happily. She seemed to be enjoying his reactions to everything.

The boy redirected his attention to the street in front of him. Everything was so vivid, the colors vibrant and the images danced in front of him. He watched as street lights entered his peripheral, flashing brightly –almost blinding the boy—before slipping out of the edge of his vision only to be replaced by the next street light. As the car slowed to a stop the boy directed his gaze up to the red light hovering above the car.

The small red dot was surrounded by an aura of light. An entire spectrum of color was visible, starting with an intense yellow, moving through the shades of orange, before finally enveloping into the red dot. The more he focused on the dot the more the boy became transfixed by it. The light changed and the new green dot was surrounded by blues and purples.

Suddenly the car lurched forward, and the beautiful sight was lost as Jfer drove through the intersection. She turned and looked at the boy with expectation.

"That was cool." Was all he could say. The colors had moved him. It almost made the boy emotional to lose the beautiful sight. Suddenly it occurred to him that there would be more stoplights on their way to the eatery. With excitement the boy sat up in his seat, and turned to smile at Jfer.

"So you like it I'm assuming?" The girl asked.

"Yeah it's beautiful really. I get what you mean by opening your mind's eye."

"Well yeah that's why it's almost impossible to explain. And everyone is affected differently so it's sometimes hard to relate even to other people's trips once you've done it yourself," said the girl.

"So what was your first trip like?"

"Horrible. I realized half-way through the trip that my boyfriend, who was literally sitting next to me, had been cheating on me," she stated in a monotone, emotionless voice.

"Damn. I'm sorry Jfer." The boy replied sincerely. He hadn't been expecting a response like this, so he snapped the rubber band against his wrist. "Wait hold on, how did you figure that out while you were tripping?"

"Well you know how it feels," Jfer responded.

"What do you mean, acid?"

"Yeah, you feel like you have to put the pieces together right? In everything. I don't know, I just started putting the pieces together that he had left me. First I started questioning the missed texts, and he tried to bullshit his way out of that. So I pushed him. I questioned him until it finally came out." Jfer took a deep breath to settle herself.

"I asked him why ever since our first date, he's had this bad habit of cancelling on me at the last minute. It was something that had always annoyed me, but I loved him and he was my guy, so I just let it go every time."

"What did he tell you?" The boy asked in a small voice.

"Well. In the nicest way possible, he explained to me how I had been his backup plan the entire time. He would make plans with me but if something came up –usually another girl—he would cancel at the last minute and spend that time with whatever prettier distraction he found."

There was a pause after Jfer said this. The boy wasn't sure how to feel. This girl who had met him no less than a couple of hours ago had kissed him, taken his cigarettes, and then admitted to him her deepest secret pretty much.

"Does this mean I'm friend-zoned or something?" The boy thought.

"Jfer, I'm so sorry. That's awful, he's got some bad karma coming for what he did"

"Yeah. Well he ended up catching chlamydia. I try not to get too worked up over it."

"Oh," was all the boy could say. Jfer was a curveball to say the least.

"Yeah, so the next day I went to Adam and tripped with him."

"So you tripped the very next day after having a bad trip your first time?" The boy asked in shock.

"Yessir," Jfer replied with a smug look on her face.

"You're crazy. You know that?" The boy asked rhetorically.

"Oh we're all crazy dude," came a voice from the back seat

The boy whipped his head around so fast he thought he might've broken his neck. He had completely forgotten Adam was sitting in the back seat and the sound of his voice had snapped the boy back into reality.

"What the fuck Adam, how long have you been back there?" The boy said before laughing at his own cluelessness.

"Oh just a minute or two, I figured I'd pop in to see how your date was going."

"Shut up asshole," Jfer said as she threw a wild punch into the backseat, just missing the side of Adam's head.

"Well excuse me, but I happen to be tripping too. It's boring enough to be stuck in the back seat, but I've had to listen to you two trying to flirt your way out of awkward situation after awkward situation all night!"

The boy and girl exchanged a puzzled look in the front seat.

"For instance." Adam continued. "Jake, I'll bet you had no idea Jfer had an ex, let alone that he cheated on her. I'm sure that makes you feel all types of hot and bothered. Now Jfer, for Christ's sake you're scaring the poor boy. Can you stop being such an emotional bitch for one minute?"

Now both parties in the front seat were offended.

"I've brought you both together tonight to share in something very special. We're at the point in the night when you two share your first dinner date. Jfer, if you'd be so kind, pull up to the window so we can order."

Both the boy and Jfer turned to look out the window, then at each other before laughing hysterically. Even Adam joined into the awkward spur-of-the-moment revelry.

Chapter 7

The "dinner date" Adam had joked about consisted of three enormous burritos, two orders of French fries, a large Dr. Pepper, and two large Sprites. The trio wolfed it all down and as the food settled, the trip came to an end for the two boys.

"Alright mama Jfer, take us home," Adam said as he rubbed his satisfied stomach and slumped into the corner of his seat.

"So is he always like this?" The boy asked Jfer.

"You mean a gigantic toddler? Playing in the sand and then wandering off until you take him for food, then once you get him food he knocks out? Oh yeah, you should see him on weekends."

"Oh I'm sure it's even funnier when he's drunk." The boy said jokingly.

"Dude you have no idea," Jfer replied as she put the key in the ignition and pulled out of the dimly-lit parking lot they had called their restaurant.

The drive back wasn't miraculous or marvelous in any sense. The boy saw everything as he had before the trip. Shitty orange street lights, annoying red lights, terrible drivers. The real world came flooding back to the boy all at once. The night was over. The grand adventure finished.

As the sun began to rise on a new day, and the sky outside went from a dark black to a dark blue the boy looked down at the time. Six O'clock it read.

"So can I drive home at this point?" The boy asked to no one in particular.

"Are the lane dividers swirly noodles?" A tired and sleepy Adam asked from the back.

"Nope. No noodles that I can see," The boy stated after looking intently at the lane dividers for a couple seconds.

"Then you're good," Adam responded with a lazy thumbs up in the boys direction.

"How reassuring," The boy muttered under his breath.

"You'll be fine," Jfer started. "If you want you can just chill with me until school starts, I'll drive you back over here and you can pick up your car after class?"

The boy thought it over for a second. Jfer was essentially inviting the boy into her house for a couple hours after her mom had already left for work. As enticing as the idea sounded he needed to go home. A shower with Jfer would be nice, but a shower by himself would be even nicer. He needed some time to collect his thoughts about the night.

"I'm good, thanks. I need to check in with my parents anyways." Was the best excuse the boy could give. He felt bad for the girl in a way. After talking all night he had learned a lot about her, and her only sibling was an older brother who went to college in Boston. Jfer had nothing to go home to. Both parents working, brother gone. The boys' home life was the polar opposite.

"Alright, Well I'll see you at school then," Jfer said with no evidence of disappointment in her voice.

The Scion pulled into the parking lot and the three deviants jumped out. With quiet and tired goodbyes Adam and Jfer got into their respective cars, and drove off. The boy took one last look at the park. The park that had been a mysterious new land just hours ago. The park that now looked just as much like a dump as it had looked every other day.

As the boy scanned the park he began to notice all the imperfections that it held. The swing that was broken and hanging by one chain, the chipping lead paint on the slides, the obvious brown spots in the grass that came from neglect by the gardeners.

After noticing all the flaws in what was once a beautiful park the boy decided he couldn't stand the sight of it anymore. He stepped into his Challenger and pulled out of the parking lot. "Heading home," the boy texted his mother while he waited at his first of many annoying red lights.

The drive home was uneventful, and when he walked in the door of his house he was able to navigate past his mother without much questioning. His story had stuck, and the woman had believed it as usual.

After realizing the time, the boy hurried into the shower. The water brought a sense of safety. He had seen so much in the past eight hours. No, the boy corrected himself, he had *felt* so much in the past eight hours. Never before had he felt so connected with his surroundings. Never before had he felt so connected to the people that surrounded him.

It wasn't that the boy was an outcast, he had some friends from school like Joe and Steve. They weren't the best of friends though. They had never opened up to the boy and the boy had never felt the need to open up to them.

That night was different though. The boy felt a connection with Adam through the trip, and especially with Jfer. Even though he hadn't shared any sad stories or deep secrets with the girl, it meant something that she had opened up to him so unconditionally. Nobody had done that before, and the boy was still not sure how he felt about the whole thing.

Next he thought of the park. How it had seemed so magical on that first night, but then in reality it was an eyesore to the general public. "Certainly not the type of place you'd want to bring children," mused the boy. After thinking about it more than he had intended, the boy decided there was nothing he could do about it, as it was someone else's job to maintain the parks of his community.

After his shower the boy threw on clothes, fixed his hair in the mirror, and hurried out the front door with a bagel in hand and a kiss from his mom on his forehead. As he stepped into the Challenger and threw his backpack in the passenger seat the boy was struck with the realization that he had left his bong in Adam's car.

It wasn't that he had a problem with Adam, especially after the night before, but he just didn't want to deal with the awkward conversation that retrieving his prized possession would require. There would be that awkward moment when they both realized they had a mutual experience that shouldn't be brought up. Then the awkwardness of walking to Adam's car and trying to keep up conversation about random things the boy really didn't care about.

The boy decided to just give it time. He hadn't planned on hanging out with Adam or Jfer at school, so he figured after a couple days the awkwardness would wear off and he could make up some terrible excuse as to why he had left the bong in Adam's car for so long.

As the boy drove to school he gradually became more and more entrapped in his thoughts about the previous night. He was almost glad when his first period teacher told everyone to take a seat.

Everything was back to normal. No spontaneous flashes of color, no patterns on the walls, nothing. It calmed the boy. The familiar feeling of apathy crept into him as he sat in the back of class. There was Jess giving Dalton her number, Ms. Walsh rambling on about global economics when she had never traveled any further than Miami for spring break '82, and there was that same sound that the boy hated most about school. The pen-clicking. For whatever reason every class had one kid that would sit there and pretend to pay attention while furiously clicking his pen.

The boy couldn't take it anymore. After one final click-click he rose from his seat, made his way across the classroom to the disapproval of Ms. Walsh, and plucked the pen from the clicker's hand. The class went silent. He set the pen on the other boys desk and marched back to his seat before plunking down and looking back at the bemused teacher staring at him from the front of class.

"Feel free to continue," The boy said casually.

"Thank you Mr. Rivera, and Mr. Winton?" The clicker looked up from his desk still partially in shock that he had just been put on blast in front of the entire class.

"Yes Ms. Walsh?" He replied quietly.

"Next time I'll take that pen myself and stick it where the sun don't shine," the teacher said with a tone that made the whole class let out a nervous laugh.

"Of course, my bad" the clicker replied as he looked down at his desk.

Ms. Walsh continued her lecture on China's strengthening market, so the boy leaned back in his chair and considered his work done for the day. He was already getting looks from some of the other kids in his class, and he began to regret making such a scene. It was odd to him, never before would he have had the confidence or balls to stand up in the middle of class and physically silence a clicker. He had always wanted to though.

After class the boy made a beeline for the door and made his way to second period without anyone from his last class talking to him about the incident. Second period was uneventful, as were most of the rest of his classes. He had seen Jfer at lunch, but made sure just to give a nod and a casual "hey" before continuing to walk past her.

By the time sixth period came around the boy was physically and mentally exhausted. He hadn't gotten any sleep the night before, so he knew a catnap was coming as soon as he entered the door for trigonometry. When he arrived to class the boy took his usual seat in the back and watched as the rest of the students filed in.

The boy was waiting for Adam to enter the door. Not because he wanted to talk to the other boy, or even sit next to him. He just wanted to see how exhausted Adam was in comparison to himself.

But Adam never showed up. The boy was worried for a second, but then after thinking about the previous night and even that morning he realized that Adam had probably just gone home and slept through school. The boy resigned himself to putting his head down on his arm and letting sleep take him. The classroom was heated due to the cold temperature outside, so the boy slipped into a doze and then a nap within minutes.

"Mr. Rivera," came a voice from out of the glorious sleep.

"Yeehzir," the boy responded as he slowly pulled himself off of the table.

"Class ended about five minutes ago. Oh and you slept through a quiz by the way."

"What? Why hell didn't you wake me up?" The boy fired at the teacher standing over him.

"Well you seemed to be having such a great dream I figured it would be a shame to wake you from it," Mr. Jensen replied with a smug look on his face.

"Jesus," the boy muttered as he rubbed his eyes. "Well can I retake it?"

"Yeah you can, don't worry. Let's go for a smoke and I'll ask you the questions off the top of my head."

"So I won't have paper to work them out?" The boy asked hesitantly.

"You shouldn't need them. Right brainchild?" The teacher responded.

"No, I'll do just as fine without scratch paper," the boy shot back confidently.

"That's what I thought, come on grab your things. I'm going to show you a safer place to smoke where you won't cause any trouble to visitors."

The boy couldn't help but laugh a little. Mr. Jensen was cool, and besides, this would give him a chance to learn more about the odd man who worked as a public school teacher.

Chapter 8

Mr. Jensen led the boy outside of the main building towards the lunch tables, just as he was getting close to the spot the boy had first seen the woman with the dragon tattoo, he veered right into a smaller doorway near the cafeteria. This doorway led into a hallway filled with retired jerseys of the great athletes that had come through the school.

The boy realized that the doors on either side of the hallways must have been the coaching offices. The jerseys lined up between each doorway seemed to point to which sport the offices were aligned with. Finally Mr. Jensen opened a door at the end of the hall which lead to daylight.

As the boy stepped out of the dimly lit hallway, he realized that he had never seen this part of the campus before. The teacher adjusted his glasses to the light and walked towards an old table and set of chairs perched in the middle of the grass courtyard. Both the boy and the teacher sat down as Mr. Jensen spoke for the first time throughout their entire trip.

"So, what do you think?" The man asked as he sparked a cigarette.

The boy took a moment to observe his surroundings.

"It's awesome," he responded, and he meant it. The courtyard was about ten yards wide and ten yards long. Almost a perfect square of green that had been squashed between two grey buildings and a football field. The grass was green, well-kept, and surrounded by beautiful rose bushes on all sides.

"It's even prettier in the springtime, when the flowers start to blossom. I call this place the secret garden," Mr. jensen explained happily.

"Do other teachers and students know about this place?" The boy asked, still surprised that he had never found this gem on his own.

"Not sure, I've never seen anybody back here and I've come out after school nearly every day for the past couple years."

"So it is a secret garden," the boy said as he lit his own cigarette and looked around again.

"Pretty much. I mean most students don't care to hang around very much after school, and it's tucked away enough that the students who do probably won't ever find it in their four years here."

"Well it's a cool spot regardless, am I allowed to come back here whenever?"

"Nope, sorry kid you need a super-secret key which only the Principal hands out."

"Wait, what?"

"I'm messing with you, of course you can come back here. I didn't show you this place so you could walk around campus smoking."

"We're still on campus Mr. Jensen," the boy replied with a smirk

"Shut up. You're a smartass you know that?"

"So I've been told," the boy said with a chuckle.

The boy really liked Mr. Jensen. The guy was smart, funny, and what other teacher would show a student a secret smoking spot? The boy decided to push his luck, and see if Mr. Jensen would open up to him as easily as Jfer had the night before.

"Just don't let me catch you smoking weed out here." Mr. Jensen added.

"Yeah about that," the boy started. "I heard you're a homie when it comes to kids getting in trouble around here?"

"What do you mean?" The teacher asked with suspicion.

"Well I heard you hid someone's backpack full of weed when he was brought up to the office." The boy said sheepishly. He didn't want to sell Adam out but he had to know more about this man smoking next to him.

"Well to tell you the truth, I've helped quite a few of my students out when it comes to sticky situations. I remember being a kid in high school. You do some stupid shit sometimes. Everyone does. I just think the way the administration handles it is totally wrong. Why would you send an eighteen-year-old kid to the police when he has a little bit of weed on him, for God's sake nearly everyone smoked at some point in their life." The man finished his rant with a question. "You know who probably smoked the most weed in high school?"

The boy looked up, puzzled by the question. "The Principal?"

"The Principal." The teacher confirmed. "And while everyone else moved on in their lives our Principal decided to stay put, in his comfortable domain, the school system."

The boy was going to ask how the teacher knew all of this, but realized he had finished his cigarette and was smoking mostly filter by that point.

"Well you'll have to tell me how you know all of this about principal McIlroy sometime." The boy stated as he pulled his backpack over his shoulders.

"Sounds good, take care of yourself Jake."

"Later Mr. Jensen."

"Oh and Jake!"

"Yes sir?"

"I'll give you an eighty on that quiz, just remember that this is a non-smoking campus." The teacher said with a smile and a half-hearted salute.

"Oh yeah! Thanks, have a good one sir." The boy replied as he turned around and walked towards the exit of the secret garden.

It took the boy no time at all to navigate his way back to the lunch tables. "Hidden in plain sight." He mused as he began the trek to his car. It was cold out, and the boy had no jacket so he moved quickly through the parking lot. On his way he noticed Adam's Scion in its usual parking spot.

The boy wondered why Adam's car was in the lot but Adam had failed to make it to class, so he took a slight detour and walked past the driver's side of the car. As he passed the driver's window he saw something that made him stop. Adams slumbering head was slumped against the window, where it seemed to have been for most of the day. A vast majority of his face was sunburnt, and he had a groove running across his cheek from where his seatbelt had been digging in.

The boy knocked on the car window with no response. Next he tried a light pounding, with still no success other than Adam tucking his head into his arm like a bird. Finally the boy decided to try the door. Luckily it was unlocked, so Adam took a little tumble out of his seat before the seatbelt caught him.

"WUAHHHH!" Adam protested as he came to his senses from the minor heart attack.

"Dude, you slept through the whole day. In the school parking lot. With my bong in your backseat." The boy replied, surprised at how genuinely concerned he was for Adam.

"Oh shut up, are you my mother?"

"No, I kind of thought that was Jfer's job to be honest." The boy said with a sly grin on his face. He couldn't help it, just saying her name aloud brought back a stream of vibrant memories from the previous night.

"This is weird," the boy thought. "First I'm checking up on Adam and trying to tell him what to do with his life, and now I'm going all giddy-schoolgirl over Jfer. I need to put an end to this."

"What's with the stupid look on your face? You know she's out of your league anyways," Adam responded, snapping the boy back into reality.

"Don't be jealous, Adam. Besides, I always try to choose fights above my bracket." The boy replied with insincere cockiness. "So I left my bong in your car, can I get that back?

"Oh yeah I broke that on accident while I was sleeping."

"You fuck! Do you know how much that cost me?" The boy began to explode.

"Just kidding calm your tits, but I'm only giving it back to you if you come to my CEO's and Corporate Hoes party next Friday," Adam responded coolly. After looking the boy up and down once more he added "Oh and make sure to dress accordingly, or at least *try*."

The boy wasn't sure what to say. On the one hand he obviously needed his bong. On the other hand he would have to deal with all of the backwards losers at his school. Even worse, he would have to deal with them being drunk.

"Come on Adam, I just need the bong."

"Nope, sorry bud, you've avoided my parties all year and now you think you can trip with me once and refuse another invitation? I don't think so."

"Alright I'll stop by, but I want that bong now so you don't break it."

"Deal," Adam replied before adding "but if you don't show up to my party I'll tell everyone at school that we hooked up and you gave me the Herps."

"Wait but then you have to say you have Herpes. How is that even a threat, you're only hurting your own rep?" The boy responded, confused at the other boys attempt at negotiating.

"Shut up and just come to my party, alright? You'll have fun I promise."

"Alright fine, I'll be there." The boy finally replied, giving in just to make the other boy happy.

"Good answer." Adam said as he reached into the back seat of the car.

Adam handed the boy the black sleeve with the glass inside and said his goodbye, adding that he couldn't wait to see the boy, with a sly wink before closing his door and starting his car.

As the Scion pulled out of the parking spot the boy turned to walk back towards his own car. The boy thought about what he had just agreed to. On the one hand he had never been to a high school party, and figured it would be best to at least check one out before graduation. If nothing else it would broaden his perspective of the other kids he saw day in and day out at school. On the other hand there was a reason he had never been to a high school party. He hated the idea of getting to know the kids at his school. He preferred the comfort of anonymity that he held towards the other students. The boy hated drama and knew that keeping himself segregated from the "popular kids" who partied was his best tactic for avoiding it.

In the end he decided to at the least make an appearance at the party. If it was as bad as he envisioned then he would find Adam and make his way back out as quickly as he had come in.

The boy had arrived at his destination, so he unlocked the Challenger and threw his backpack in the passenger seat and his black sleeve in the back. He then walked back around to the driver's side, opened the door, and fell down and back into his seat. After closing the door he turned the key in the ignition and pulled out of the spot.

The boy once again couldn't help but look over at the park as he drove past it. Memories began to flow through his mind as he recalled his childhood. The days when his mother would pick him up early from school and take him to the park. The boy would have the playground all to himself since the other children were in school learning the alphabet and simple addition. His mother had her own methods of teaching the boy. One time she gave him a crispy and dried-out leaf that had fallen from one of the trees, and told him to go find another exactly like it. After the boy had tired himself out scavenging the park for an identical leaf the mother explained that leaves are like people. Just like how there are no two leaves identical in the park, no two people are exactly the same.

The memory brought a smile to the boy. He had continued to believe this metaphor taught by his mother until high school. On the first day the boy was thrown into a sea of fish, and try as he might he couldn't fit in with any one social group. He began to see similarities between them, and after isolating himself from the social caste system as a whole, he had begun to see just how extraordinarily similar everyone was. Everybody dressed like each other, acted like each other, and tried so hard to fit in and be exactly like each other.

That was the day the boy realized his mother was wrong. Deep down every human may have subtle differences, but even deeper than that at the heart of every human is the desire to feel accepted. In high school kids would do anything to be accepted, they yearned for acceptance; to be considered "normal." This primal drive to be accepted by peers led to the shedding of one's individuality, the boy thought. He remembered after just one month into freshman year he had decided he wanted no part of the sick game. He wouldn't break his individuality just to be considered another fish in the sea.

The boy knew his potential. While he had no idea what he would do with his life, he knew that he would not waste his life doing the exact same thing that any other monkey with a college degree could do. He would not break. He would not break for acceptance in high school, and he would not break for acceptance in society. The thought of a nine-to-five job repulsed him.

As all of these thoughts raced through the boy's head the Challenger continued to race down the road. The boy jumped onto the freeway, dodged his way through traffic, and exited back off the freeway. He enjoyed the rush of flying through traffic, swerving around slow drivers and tearing past timid ones. The speed and manner with which he drove forced the boy to focus on the road, allowing a break from his constant stream of racing thoughts. Driving offered the boy a sense of calm. He had read stories of experienced fighters who believe there is nothing more calming than a scrap. Any time your body is pumping adrenaline through your veins it forces your thoughts to slow down and your reflexes to quicken. Driving 110 miles per hour through light traffic certainly had the effect of pumping adrenaline into the boy's veins.

Before he knew it the boy had arrived at his house. He pulled into the driveway, threw the Challenger in park, grabbed his backpack from the passenger seat, and stepped out of the car. Making his way towards the front door the boy hit the lock button on his keys, and slung the pack over his back.

As he walked through the house, following his usual routine, he noticed something was different. His mother was nowhere to be found. The boy walked out to the garage and saw that the woman's car was gone, so he assumed she was out running errands or perhaps at the gym. Putting no unnecessary amount of thought into the situation, the boy quickly walked outside and smoked a joint before falling back into routine and taking his after-school nap to music.

Chapter 9

As the Challenger pulled into Adam's neighborhood the boy was struck by just how many other cars were parked along the street. He was still a block away from Adams house. Could all of these people be going there? A glance to his right gave him the answer he was looking for, a group of girls dressed for a party walked down the sidewalk. Each one was trying to cover the bottle of alcohol clearly sticking out of their bag.

"What the hell have I gotten myself into?" The boy muttered to himself as he parallel parked behind a jeep.

As the boy stepped out of the car he noticed the sticker on the back of the Jeep was the logo for a different high school in the area. The boy didn't think much of it and instead grabbed a couple prerolleds from his center console, shut the door, locked the car, and began making his way down the street.

"What the fuck. Is that Jake Rivera?"

"No way, I've never seen him at a party."

The boy tried to ignore the girls walking behind him, but they clearly had no consideration for him. Or perhaps they were too stupid to realize he was only a few steps ahead of them.

"I heard he dropped acid at the park the other night."

"By himself? What a freak."

The boy had finally had enough, he wasn't halfway to the party and these girls were already giving him shit. He decided to handle this in the most courteous way possible.

"Excuse me ladies," the boy said as he turned around to face them.

"Oh, hi. Are you going to Adams?" One of the girls asked sheepishly. She was tall, skinny, and blonde. The girl would have been beautiful if it weren't for the trashy extensions she wore which didn't match with the natural color of her hair.

"Yeah, actually I am. I tripped with him and Jfer the other night and now I apparently owe him by going to one of his parties."

"Oh, yeah Adam does that sometimes," the blonde said with a nervous laugh.

"Listen girls, I don't really want to be here, but I made a deal with Adam. So here's the deal, if you want to talk shit behind my back. Feel free to, because I really couldn't care less. Just so you know though, talking behind someone's back doesn't mean you LITERALLY talk about them when they're four fucking steps in front of you."

The girls were in shock. The boy wondered if any guy had ever talked to them like that before. He didn't know what to expect as a response. Maybe they'd brush him off, walk past and quietly insult him as they did. Or maybe they were the kind of girls to get in his face for calling them out on their shit talking. After a long and slightly uncomfortable pause the shorter brunette next to the blonde spoke up.

"Damn, looks like somebody needs a shot or three."

The girls began laughing as the boy stood tense with uncertainty. He wasn't sure if she was being a sarcastic bitch or just pulling his leg.

"Hi, I'm Amanda," the brunette said as she walked up to the boy and handed him a flask.

"Jake," the boy replied, still unsure of the girls intentions.

"I know, we've had like two classes together every year since middle school," the girl said as if the boy was stupid for not remembering in the moment every person he ever had classes with.

"Oh of course, Amanda Alanos! I couldn't forget such a pretty face," the boy quickly recovered.

"Wow. Thanks, I guess." The girl said as she pulled the hair out of her face and looked down at the ground with a smile.

The boy uncapped the flask and took a whiff of what was inside.

"Whiskey?" He asked with a smile.

"Jack Tennessee Honey," Amanda replied proudly.

"Good choice," the boy responded as he took a swig of the cool liquid. It burned as it slid down his throat, but he knew better than to make a face in front of girls.

"You can hold onto that, I've got the rest of the bottle in my bag," Amanda said happily as she began walking in the direction of the party.

The boy turned to follow her but stopped halfway and turned back to the rest of the girls.

"Hi there, so obviously you all know my name, but I don't think I've met any of you."

The blonde introduced herself first as Whitney before turning and introducing the other two girls as Gabi and Alex.

"Nice to meet you," the boy said with a smile before turning and following Amanda towards the party.

The night was chilly and the boy hadn't thought to bring a jacket, so as he caught up to Amanda he took another sip from the flask. The alcohol warmed his insides and made the cool night air a little more tolerable.

Amanda moved in a little closer to the boy so that the two were rubbing arms with each stride.

"So Jake, why haven't I ever seen you at parties?" The girl inquired.

"I don't know, I haven't been to many. As a matter of fact this is my first one."

"You've never been to a party before?" Amanda asked with a serious tone in her voice.

"Nope, never wanted to get stuck DDing and never wanted to have to deal with a bunch of drunk high school students. I've seen enough of my family drunk to know it's more annoying than anything else."

"Well were you sober all those times with your family?"

"Yeah."

"Well there's your problem. Go ahead and take another sip of that whiskey. The only time drunk people are fun to be around is when you're drunk too," Amanda said as she looked up at the boy with a smirk.

"Oh really? Well I can't argue with that logic," the boy said before taking another swig. He figured if he was already having enough of a good time with these girls, then the party itself couldn't be that bad. Maybe he would even enjoy himself.

The boy had his hands in his pockets to keep them warm, so he was caught off-guard when Amanda looped her arm around his and grabbed onto his elbow.

"Damn girl, your hands are freezing!" The boy said as he shot a grin at the girl.

"Oh sorry!" She replied with a laugh. Her hand stayed in place though, and she dug her nails into the boy's arm and shot him a wink.

The boy looked up and smiled. He liked high school parties already, and he hadn't even been to one yet.

As the group approached the house Amanda and the rest of the girls pulled the bottles out of their bags and led the way over the lawn to the front door. A line of guys were waiting outside, but Amanda pulled the boy up to the front with her.

"Hey Steven!" She said to the boy manning the door.

"What's up Amanda, sorry dude, its three bucks at the door for guys, you're going to have to wait in line too."

The boy realized the doorman was addressing him, so he scrounged around his pockets looking for a wallet. Before he could detach himself from Amanda to walk to the back of the line, the girl piped up.

"Oh come on Steven, it's Jakes first party and he showed up with four bad bitches and bottles. Cut the kid some slack."

Steven finally seemed to realize who the boy was.

"Wait. Jake? Jake Rivera?" With a laugh the other boy continued, "What a trip! Adam didn't think you were going to show! Come on in man, you don't have to pay."

Amanda turned and smiled at the boy before taking his hand and leading him in the door.

"Thanks Steven," the boy called back as he followed the girl inside.

He wasn't sure if the other boy had replied or not, because as soon as he entered the house he was surrounded by noise. A DJ was in the front room of the house blasting loud rap music for the party denizens to dance to. All the lights in this room were off, except for a small light show projector placed hanging from the chandelier. Spinning red and green dots were being cast over everyone in the room. Some people were dancing, but most were trying to talk over the music, which created a mishmash of sounds. As Amanda pulled the boy deeper into the party he caught parts of people's conversations mixed in with lyrics from the music.

"So do you go to Aruba-"

"SOMEBODY SAY AYYYYYE WE WANT SOME-"

"Is that Jake Rivera?"

After making it through the front room, Amanda and the boy reached the kitchen and a small living room. The lights were on in this room and it was a little quieter. Amanda stopped at a couple of bar stools by the island and sat down, prompting the boy to sit next to her.

"You have that deer in the headlights look, it's adorable." Amanda said with a laugh.

The boy opened his eyes as wide as he could and began frantically looking around the room. This prompted the girl to laugh even harder, and as she doubled over she reached her hand out and caught the boys forearm.

"Yeah well it's definitely a lot more than I expected," the boy said before leaning back in his seat.

"Oh yeah, Adam goes all out. His parents let him do this as long as everyone has a driver or crashes here."

"Really? That's nuts, my parents would never let something like this happen." The boy replied in surprise.

"Yeah, I mean when you think about it, it's a pretty smart way to handle it. Your kids are going to party and drink anyways, so why not have them do it in your own house so you can control the environment?"

"You call that control?" The boy said as he pointed to a drunk guy outside. The boy watched as the other guy leaned too far into a table, causing it to slide away from him. As the table slid the guy toppled over onto the ground. Instead of picking himself up and brushing himself off like any normal person would do, the guy sat up and began laughing at himself.

"Well, no. But here comes the control now," Amanda replied as she turned back and nodded her head in the direction behind the boy.

The boy turned to see a man in his early fifties with a white pony tail and beard walking through the party. The man shot a look of pure ice to Amanda before stepping outside and picking the drunkard up off the ground. One of the other guys standing around helped the man pick the kid up, and walked him over to a seat. The man gave a quick word to the drunk one in the seat, then turned to the one that had helped him and had a quick inaudible conversation. Afterwards the man patted the drunk kid on the shoulder, and began walking around the backyard.

"Was that Mr. King?" The boy asked Amanda.

"Yep, he's the one who keeps us in line around here. Adam's mom usually posts up with the stoners in the garage."

"Adam's mom smokes?" The boy was amazed. Never before had he seen or heard of parents as cool as Adams.

"Yeah, she's such a cute little hippie-mom. You'll get to know both of them if you hang out here more often."

"Something tells me I'll be coming to a lot more of Adam's parties from now on." The boy said before looking up at the girl and smiling.

For a moment neither of them spoke, their eyes were locked and both of them were smiling. The boy was the one who broke the silence.

"So do you smoke?" He asked as he pulled the pack of cigarettes out of his pocket.

"Only when I'm drunk." Amanda replied with a playful grin.

"So we should take a couple shots then?"

"You learn quickly don't you?" Said the girl as she pulled the bottle of jack from her bag. "Here's the thing though, we don't take shots. We take pulls."

"Pulls?" The boy asked inquisitively.

Instead of answering the boy Amanda uncapped the bottle and put it up to her lips. She tipped the bottle vertically and chugged on it for a solid ten seconds before setting it down. With a shake of her head and a laugh she passed the bottle to the boy.

"That's a pull." Amanda declared proudly.

"Jesus Christ you're an alcoholic." The boy said with a nervous laugh. He had never seen his family members drink like that before.

"Excuse me! I prefer to be called a binge-drinker. It's not alcoholism until you graduate college."

"Oh is that what you tell yourself?" The boy asked sarcastically.

"No, but what eighteen year old wants to think of themselves as an alcoholic?" She replied defensively.

"Fair enough," the boy offered before taking a pull of his own.

The first sip was awful. The boy's throat felt like it was on fire, but he pressed on and tipped the bottle vertical just as Amanda had done and continued chugging. After the first sip it became easier to drink, and he made sure to stop after eleven seconds before setting the bottle back down.

The boy suppressed his urge to vomit and instead took a deep breath before mentioning the fact that he had taken a longer pull than the girl. Amanda laughed at this and said something about how the boy would definitely be having a good time tonight.

After two shorter pulls, they walked to the backyard and found a quiet place to sit and smoke. The boy offered the girl a cigarette and lit it for her before putting his own to his lips and sparking it. After a moment of silence Amanda said something that caught the boy by surprise.

"You know Jake, nobody hates you."

"What?" The boy asked in shock.

"Well you've always acted like you had this chip on your shoulder. Like everybody hates you, but in reality you're not that bad of a guy."

"Wow. I'm not sure whether to be offended or take the compliment," the boy replied cynically.

"See that's what I'm talking about, you have this attitude like everyone's always trying to diss you. In reality nobody cares enough to single you out. You've never done anything to get made fun of, but you just don't go out of your way to be friendly."

"Okay now I'm really confused."

"Take the other day in Ms. Walsh's class for example. When Chris Winton was clicking his pen constantly, and nobody was doing shit about it. You literally stepped up and shut him up in front of the entire class. You acted like it was no big deal but that was one of the funniest and coolest things I've seen in a while."

"Oh. Well thanks, that kid was annoying the shit out of me that's all."

"Yeah, he was annoying the shit out of everyone."

"Are you trying to make a point? Or just rambling?" The boy asked. He wasn't sure if Amanda was drunk and talking to talk, or sincerely meant all of this.

"My point is, don't be so hard on everyone else, and don't be so hard on yourself. People enjoy having you around, it'd be nice if you returned the favor by enjoying other people."

"Well I'm certainly enjoying you so far tonight." The boy said with a flirtacious bump against the girl.

"Why did I say that?" He thought instantly. "I've never pulled a line like that off before, I guess they call alcohol liquid courage for a reason." Amanda broke him from his thoughts.

"Oh shut up!" She said with a laugh as she pushed him.

"Sorry, couldn't help it," the boy replied with a giddy grin.

"Alright, well how's about we start by dancing. Can you walk newbie?" The girl asked as she put out her cigarette and stood up.

"Oh please." The boy said as he pushed himself up off the ledge.

As soon as the boy stood up straight the alcohol hit him like a bag of bricks. His knees buckled and he swayed, and he had to shuffle his feet around to keep upright. Amanda giggled as she watched him.

"What are you laughing at?" The boy said as he stepped in closer to the girl.

"You look like Bambi." The girl said with a laugh before turning towards the door.

Amanda led the boy back inside the house, and into the room with the DJ. The green and red lights were spinning and crossing over the crowd of teens. The boy realized at this point that he was significantly tipsy. Not drunk yet, but the tipsiest he had ever been.

The girl took the boy into the middle of the crowd and began to dance. The loud bumping bass of the music combined with the lubricant of alcohol turned the boy into a much better dancer than he thought he was. At some point Amanda turned around and the boy grabbed her hips and pulled her back against him.

The two danced like this for some time, occasionally Amanda would turn around to kiss the boy. "If this is how easy high school parties are I'm the stupidest man alive for not doing this earlier," the boy thought.

Eventually the DJ changed the tempo and began playing trap music and techno, which turned the dance floor into a jumping and grinding frenzy. The man behind the turntables would sometimes throw confetti or baby powder out into the crowd as the beat dropped, causing the drunken teens to go even crazier.

"Jake!" a girl's voice broke out through the crowd.

The boy continued dancing with Amanda while scanning the crowd for the face he was looking for. Finally he spotted Jfer a few feet away smiling at him. She was dancing with a different guy, but stepped away from him to walk over to the boy. He backed off of Amanda and waved Jfer over.

"Jake! Holy shit I didn't know you were coming tonight!" Jfer said excitedly.

"Well yeah, Adam convinced me!" The boy exclaimed, trying to be heard over the music and mob of people.

"Pretty dope, huh?" Jfer said smugly.

"Yeah, I'm definitely coming to the rest of these from now on."

"Hey Amanda, can I steal Jake real quick, I want to show Adam he came through."

Amanda gave the boy a look before telling Jfer it was fine. The boy leaned in and told the girl he'd find her in a little bit, before turning to follow Jfer out of the crowd.

After getting through the mob of people in the front room, Jfer stopped and turned to the boy.

"So Amanda got you to drink with her I'm assuming?"

"Yeah I took a couple pulls," The boy replied.

"Wow, okay you're holding up really well then. Good shit Jake."

"To be honest I've never actually been drunk before. I have to say it's a nice feeling."

"Oh buddy if you aren't stumbling around yet then you aren't actually drunk. You're a little tipsy that's all. But I'm glad you like it, I prefer drugs obviously but that's for my own reasons."

"And what reasons are those?" The boy asked.

"My bitch of a mother," Jfer said with a smile before turning back and heading towards the garage.

The boy took his steps carefully. He knew he wasn't about to fall into something, but the combination of alcohol plus dancing had made his legs feel like wet noodles. When they reached the garage Jfer turned to the boy and told him to stay inside for a second.

A moment after Jfer closed the garage door behind her Adam came barging through it, eyes wide with excitement.

"JAKE!" He exclaimed ecstatically before wrapping the boy in a bear hug. "Dude I honestly didn't think you were coming!"

"Oh what and miss this? Come on." The boy said in amusement as he pulled himself away from his friend.

"So you're having a good time then?" Adam asked with a smile and diamonds in his eyes.

"Yeah I'm having a great time actually, thanks for having me man."

"No problem, glad you're enjoying yourself. Hey you need to come outside and meet the squad!"

So the boy followed Adam into the garage and sat down in the stoner circle. Out in the garage it was a little colder than inside the house, but the music wasn't nearly as loud so the boy decided to stay and sober up before heading back inside.

Each member of the so-called "squad" introduced themselves, until finally Adam's mother stood from her chair to shake the boy's hand. Kelly King was in her early sixties and had the body of a female athlete. She was lean and tan with bleach blonde hair that shot out in every direction around her narrow face. After introducing himself to Mrs. King the boy whipped out one of his prerolled joints and asked the group if they wanted to smoke. Jfer instantly put down the bowl she was packing and snatched the joint from the boy's hand.

"Bitch." The boy said as he shot the girl a look.

"Just be thankful Amanda isn't out here. She would've pocketed it and be walking back to the car by now." Jfer replied with a smirk.

"Oh-ho-ho-ho, wait what about Amanda?" Adam asked as he leaned forward in his seat, suddenly interested in the conversation.

"Jake was trying to hit that. Sexually." Jfer said, bringing laughter to the group and causing the boy to fluster even more.

"Not even, we were just dancing." He said defensively.

"After she pumped you full of booze. You got to be careful kiddo that girl is like a spider, she'll hit you with the venom then eat you alive."

"Come on. She seemed like a nice girl!" The boy retorted.

"So, how many people in here have hooked up with Amanda Alanos?" Jfer called out to the group.

Almost every hand in the group went up, including a couple girls and Adam's mother.

"Mrs. King?" The boy asked incredulously.

"Nah hun, I'm just fucking with you." She said with a laugh.

The boy laughed back nervously. There were a lot of hands up, at least six different guys and two girls. He was starting to see the problem, but Jfer wasn't finished yet.

"And how many people have been fucked over by Amanda Alanos?" She asked again to the group.

This time every single hand went up.

"She's gotten drunk and called the cops on this place twice after we sent her home." Stated Mrs. King. "I told Adam if it happens again we won't be letting her in anymore."

"Okay so you're telling me I shouldn't hook up with Amanda." The boy said stupidly.

"No, we're telling you to give her three children and buy a house for her." Jfer replied sarcastically while passing the joint to the boy.

"Got it." He said as he plucked the rolled up misdemeanor from Jfer's hand and took a hit.

"So mom" Adam began. "Jake's the one I was telling you about last week, remember the one who I got to trip for the first time with Jfer and I at the park?"

The boy was mid-hit when Adam had said this and the surprise made him sit up in his seat and hack up smoke.

"Good times! How'd you like it hun?" Mrs. King asked the boy as if it was no big deal. The boy had officially come to the decision that he loved this place, and loved these people.

Not sure of what to say, he chose his words carefully.

"It was fun, I mean nothing like what I expected. I had a lot more control over it than I thought I would."

"Oh just wait until you take a ten strip. The idea of control goes straight out the window." Mrs. King said with a laugh.

The rest of the squad laughed in agreement. The boy was beginning to realize that this was the druggie circle, and he felt very out of place. He passed the joint to the girl on his left, who had introduced herself as Maria.

"So I'm sorry, I'm a bit new to psychedelics and partying counter-culture. But Mrs. King, you have to be the chillest Mom I've ever met." The boy said.

"Oh well thanks hun! I'm flattered. But don't worry you'll get used to people like us. Just do me a favor and don't ever use the word counter-cultural. It reminds me of my father back when I was a free-spirited sixteen year-old." The woman replied with a laugh.

"Sorry, I'll make sure to keep that in mind." The boy said with a chuckle.

The boy was starting to feel the effects of mixing alcohol with weed. So after thanking the Kings for having him, he excused himself from the group and made his way back into the house. His first stop was the bathroom, after waiting approximately twenty minutes to get in the door he purged himself of the last remnants of dinner and whiskey. After washing his mouth and splashing water on his face the boy stood up straight, looking at himself in the mirror.

His face was pale and gaunt. Beads of sweat had begun to form in the corners of his forehead and his hands were trembling. It dawned on the boy that he would have to drive home sometime soon, so he decided to make his way out of the bathroom and back towards the kitchen. The boy received looks from a few of the people he passed, but kept his head down to avoid talking to people with his puke-breath.

Once he had arrived in the kitchen he grabbed an unopened water bottle off the counter and made his way back outside to post up on the same ledge he had visited earlier with Amanda. Throwing up most of the whiskey had sobered him up some, and sipping the water helped to relieve the disgusting taste of bile in the back of the boy's throat. After a few deep breaths he pulled out a cigarette, put it to his lips and lit it. Just as he took his first drag a familiar voice came from his right.

"I hope you planned on deucing that with me."

The boy looked up to see Amanda casually strolling over to him. She looked just as frazzled as the boy did, and he noticed she had lost the jacket she had been wearing earlier in the night.

"Funny, the girl who got me fucked up at my first high school party is asking to split a cigarette with me now. You do know I have to drive home at some point right?" The boy spat as he shot the girl a look of resentment.

"Ouch. I expected a little more gratitude newbie. After all, I did get you fucked up at your first high school party." As Amanda said this she sat down on the boy's lap, gave him a look of pure fire, and stole the cigarette from his hands.

"God you are just the perfect girl to bring home to momma aren't you?" The boy said sarcastically. He had understood the point Jfer was trying to make in the garage about Amanda, but something about the girl's curves, curls, and crazy-eyes had the boy hooked.

"Oh honey, I'm the girl your momma prays for every night." Amanda replied as she took a drag of the cigarette, pushed the boy's lips to her own, and exhaled smoke down his throat.

The smoke singed his throat and he would've started coughing, but the taste of Amanda's lips on his own kept him locked in place. He exhaled the smoke back out his nose and pulled away from the girl. After a sip of his water the boy grabbed the cigarette from Amanda and took another drag.

"Somebody tastes like recycled whiskey," she said as she pulled a stick of gum from her bag.

"Sorry about that. Even though it is your fault," the boy fired back as he unwrapped the gum and tossed it into his mouth. "Bitch."

"Well aren't you just as sweet as a peach. Do you talk to momma that way too?"

The boy decided he had had enough of the pointless banter. He may have been going against Jfer's advice, and Amanda may have been one of the sluttiest girls he had ever met, but she was hot, and he figured a good night could only get better if he found a room for the two of them.

"I think you should show me the rest of the house." The boy proposed.

"Is that so? Well what haven't you seen yet that is so enticing?" Amanda replied.

"How's about a quiet room upstairs. They have those here right?"

"I'm sure we could find one. If not we'll make a closet work." The girl said as she hopped off the boy's lap and dragged him off his ass. The boy barely had time to grab his water and step on his cigarette before he was being led back into the house.

"A closet?" He asked incredulously.

Amanda had no reply, instead she turned back towards the boy and gave him a look that put more than a little pep in his step. He hurried to catch up to the girl as she moved through the house and led the way to the stairs. As they began taking the stairs two at a time the boy looked back down at the living room. Jfer was sitting in a chair next to a guy who seemed way more interested in her than she was in him. The guy was saying something to her, but Jfer didn't seem to care. Her eyes were locked on the boy. As soon as he locked eyes with her the girl shot him an unenthusiastic wink before looking back at the guy trying desperately to catch her attention.

Chapter 10

In complete darkness the boy was led to the bed by the girl. She pulled him on top of her and leaned up for a kiss. This kissing was different from before. Almost maniacal. A frenzy of tongue touching and lip biting. The whiskey pumping through the boys system made him feel unstoppable, even though reality wouldn't allow him to stand at attention.

As the clothes came off the curves of the girl's body were revealed in a whole different way. Hands ran up and down as the most primal human craving was being satiated. Nails were dug into skin so deep that scratches would be left for days. It wasn't the boy's first time, but this kind of sex was alien to him. Drunken, cross-faded, stupid, reckless sex. The kind of sex that you regret the next day but in the moment is the most adrenaline-fueled instinctual process humans are capable of.

The darkness revealed a sense of freedom that entranced the boy. There was no judgment, no sense of commitment, just the apathetic enjoyment of two hormone-driven fiends. Nothing was going to be the same for the boy. First the trip, then the party, and now the ultimate satisfaction of stupid drunk sex. Things were going to change for the boy. And while he didn't consciously know it as he pulled his clothes back on, there was something deep within him that was different. For the first time in a long time, the boy was able to connect with people. He had connected emotionally with Jfer at the park. He had connected mentally with Mr. Jensen after being shown the smoking garden at school. He had connected sexually with Amanda after a drunken night of socializing. Socializing at a party no less! A first for the boy.

The night ended soon after the trip to the bedroom, so the boy made sure to say his goodbyes and thanked the King family for having him before heading to his car. After smoking in the garage and exercising in the bedroom he had sobered up enough to drive home. As far as the boy was concerned he wouldn't have any trouble with police so long as he drove safely.

After the cautious fifteen minute drive home the boy slipped into his house quietly to find his parents waiting for him in the kitchen. It was obvious they had waited up for him most of the night.

"So where did you end up going tonight?" His father began, sizing the boy up and scanning almost as if he could sense the change in his son.

"My friend Adam's house. He had a couple of kids from school over so we were just hanging out."

"Was it a party?" His mother asked in a tone suggesting she already assumed it was a party.

"No, not really. There was only like six of us there. I met this girl named Amanda so I was just talking to her most of the night."

The boy's father chimed in again at this point. "Talking huh? Is that why you reek of latex and sweat?" He said with a cheeky grin in the boy's direction.

"WESTLEY." The mother said in shock as she shot the father a look of disapproval. "Uncalled for. Now Jake walk that straight line down the hallway and go to sleep. We'll talk in the morning."

"Alright, well night guys, see you in the morning." The boy said as he carefully chose his steps down the hallway. He had done this walk a hundred times before while his parents observed from behind. Most of the time he had been sober or high when they made him do it, but after driving home he was sober enough to handle a straight line.

When he reached his room the boy crashed down onto the bed and reminisced on his mental timeline of the night. He had enjoyed Amanda's company, not nearly as much as he had enjoyed Amanda's body, but he would certainly make a point to talk to the girl at school during the coming week.

"Strange." The boy thought. Two weeks ago he never would've talked to Amanda, probably wouldn't have even known who she was. Now all of a sudden he felt the urge to talk to her. The boy still hadn't realized just how much he had already changed, or how much he was still going to change. However, he was beginning to notice differences in his behavior, thoughts, and emotions towards other people.

The boy didn't think it was a negative type of change in his life. After all, he did have a great time at the party and was going to make sure to attend more of Adam's social gatherings. But it was definitely change. Three weeks ago he would've laughed at the idea of going to a high school party and enjoying himself. But in that moment, as he lay in bed surrounded by his thoughts and memories from the night, he couldn't understand why he hadn't gone to a party sooner. As the final effects of the alcohol slowly seeped out of the boy's soul, he slipped into a state of sleep that surrounded him in warmth and comfort.

A girl was running ahead of the boy. He looked around and couldn't see anything she would need to run from, so he decided to give chase and see where the girl was tearing off to.

After a short time he caught up to the girl. The boy reached out to grab her shoulder but before he could she stopped abruptly and whirled around to face him.

"You didn't learn the first time." She said. The boy was too distracted to try and understand what she could've possibly meant by that. This was by far the most beautiful woman he had ever seen, like a model straight out of magazines. Yet, somehow there was something familiar about the curve of her cheekbones, the way her eyes danced across the boy's face, observing and analyzing every minute detail.

"You didn't learn the first time. Keep up." She repeated before turning back around and picking up her pace.

Confused didn't begin to describe the boy. He had nowhere else to go in the vast desert so he decided to push his luck and follow the white rabbit. The woman led him through the hot orange sand, finally stopping at a large dune.

"Why'd we stop?" The boy asked as he scanned his surroundings. Sand stretched on for as far as he could see. The landscape reminded him of the Saharan desert. He began to wonder just how the hell he had ended up here in a dream.

"You didn't learn. This time, you actually need to learn from him. He is very wise."

"Who didn't I learn from? I have absolutely no fucking idea what you're talking about lady. Mind clueing me in?"

The woman didn't respond, instead she turned and pointed back to the dune that the two had stopped in front of. There in front of the boy's eyes, came a figure he had never wanted to see, and thought he would ever have to see again. This figure had given the boy mixed emotions for years. This figure had once terrorized the boys' dreams. But then again, this was the same figure that had given the boy hope so long ago. This was the figure that had killed the boy in his dream all that time ago.

"Michael. What are you doing here? What am I doing here?" The questions racing through his head nearly made the boy's eyes spin in their sockets.

"You already know the answer to both of those questions. You need a re-do. I tried giving you what you wanted already, but you never really learned from that did you?" As Michael said this he slowly moved towards the boy. He looked just as the boy remembered, sandy blonde hair which haphazardly fell in all directions, a five o'clock shadow which had always made him seem older and wiser than the boy. Even the brown leather motorcycle jacket that he wore was something straight out of the boy's memories.

"How is this possible?" The boy was in a state of shock.

"Focus Jake! Where are you right now?" Michael didn't seem to have time for bullshit at this point.

"I, I don't fucking know, the Saharan desert or some shit?"

"No, Jake. Focus. Stop thinking for one second and feel it out. Where are you right now?"

The boy remembered this. Michael had fed him this exact same line after killing the boy in a previous dream.

"I'm dreaming."

"Good Jake, so you remember how this works right, don't let the dream slip, but don't take control. You'll lose me if you try going lucid. Just accept it. Where are we?"

"My bed."

"That's right Jake. Now you have to listen to me this time, I don't know if I can make a third guest appearance in your dreams."

"What? But why not? Where are you now?"

"Shut up Jake we don't have time. You're going to do something big. I don't know what it is yet, but you need to remember that you can handle anything. Keep calm, feel things out, and stay focused. You can handle anything."

"Okay, but wait, why did it take you like three years to come back?"

"Honestly I don't know kid. I haven't popped up in any other dreams as far as I know. Just remember what I told you." With that, Michael stepped past the boy and whispered a few words into the ear of the woman behind him.

"So where do you go after this?" The boy asked in a quiet voice. He knew his cousin was leaving soon, and he knew that this could be the last the boy ever saw of him.

"Look at you with the stereotypical questions. Come on Jake you've seen the movies. I can't tell you that. Besides, I don't even know. I'm not a ghost Jake, just a figure projected by your subconscious."

It made sense to the boy, he couldn't possibly be seeing his cousin's ghost. Yet the thought of that comforted the boy much more than the idea of his mind just playing tricks on him.

"Hey Jake, where are you?" Michael asked one final time.

"In bed." The boy said with a smile.

Chapter 11

"Jake! Come on sleepy- head get your ass out of bed."

The boy peeked open one eye to see his mother standing above him. It had been three weeks since the dream with Michael, and since then the boy's life had changed drastically. He wasn't sure if having a solid friend group around him was the "something big" that his cousin had mentioned, or if there was something even bigger still to come. Regardless, being inducted into the "garage squad"—as they were titled in his group message—was something he had been looking forward to every day since the first party he went to at Adam's house.

It was Friday, the day the group was to leave for their bi-annual camping trip. Adam's parents owned a plot of land in the local mountain range, but since they were true hippies at heart, the couple had never developed or built on the land. Instead, they had been taking Adam on camping trips in their four acres every couple of months since he was a child.

When Adam became a teenager and grew into a group of friends that shared some common illicit activities as the parents, the couple decided to let Adam have free reign of the land, so long as he didn't burn it down or build on it. Since that day when Adam was sixteen, the "squad" as they so called themselves, made it a tradition to take two trips a year for a weekend of camping in the forest. The first trip of the year usually took place in February or March, when the air was still crisp but the teens were kept warm from the spring sun. The second excursion was always carried out in the last full week of summer vacation. The teens would be able to hike to a lake nearby and rent a boat or jet skis.

As the years went by and the squad grew in number, each new member would be "initiated" during the next trip to Adam's property. The boy was to be initiated just three weeks after meeting the squad during the spring trip to the mountains. The group kept their lips sealed as to what grueling initiation acts he would be put through, but the boy imagined it would be similar to the hazing found at many college fraternities.

With all of this in mind the boy sprung from his bed at once and turned off the chiming alarm clock.

"Sorry mom, I snoozed it and passed right back out again."

"It's fine, good dream?" The mother responded with a smile.

"Eh. I didn't really sleep much. Kind of nervous about the big camping trip this weekend."

"Oh come on hun, those kids are great and you get along really well with them! And hey don't forget you're an Eagle Scout. If nothing else you can impress them with your camping and survival skills," his mother said with a wink.

This brought a smile to the boy's face. He loved his mother. She was always an optimist, and yet completely oblivious to the boy's life all at once. He had introduced Adam and Jfer to her a few days after the party and his mother had fallen in love with both of them. Slowly the rest of the squad began coming over to meet the parents and have hookah sessions in the backyard. They all seemed to love his mom, and his mom had stated several times about how much she loved all of them.

The boy's father on the other hand, wasn't quite as enthralled by the group. He had never before seen his son belong and connect with a group of friends, and while he didn't know what the reasoning for it now was, he suspected something was different about his son. However, after seeing how happy the boy was with his friends, the father decided it was best to not protest.

When the boy first approached his parents with the idea of the camping trip, they asked more questions than criminal interrogators, but the boy had his story set in stone. Every year the senior class planned their senior ditch day together. This year the class had selected a Tuesday in the spring that would come after a teacher inservice on Monday. A teacher inservice meant the students only had to email each teacher requesting a copy of their current grade in the class, so going to school was completely unnecessary.

The planning of this senior skip day had come largely from Adam, as he knew that every senior would love a four day weekend, and it was right around the time that the squad was planning to take their spring camping trip.

After explaining the whole story to his parents they had given him the dreaded "We'll talk about it," response. This usually meant the two would neglect to talk about it until the boy brought it up again, which normally sparked a debate between the parents about whether or not he should be granted permission for whatever he had asked for.

Luckily this time the parents made their decision prior to the boy having to ask again, and informed him of their decision by surprising him with a new four-person tent after school one day. The boy had been both shocked and elated, and believed his parents had finally begun to treat him as an adult.

"If becoming an adult comes with a free tent, I might actually enjoy this shit." The boy had mused that day after thinking it all through.

Within a week he had packed and prepared himself in every way possible for the trip. In one bag he had phone chargers and other forms of electronics, in another bag he had clothes, an extra blanket, and a pillow, and in a third bag he packed toiletries, two handles of alcohol, a half ounce of weed, and a book on meditation and relaxation.

While he had no idea what was waiting for him up in the mountains, the boy assumed that drugs, drinking, and sex would all be included in his time there. In order to prepare himself the boy had done a complete cleanse of his system. He hadn't smoked, drank, or taken anything in two weeks. He was going to the gym twice a day, and eating healthier than ever. The boy wanted his body to be fully prepared for what was to come, so that even if he wasn't mentally prepared, he would make it easier on himself by being physically prepared.

The boy reminisced on all of this lead-up to the weekend during his morning shower. After which, he made sure to review the plan with his mother one more time over breakfast.

"Okay so you'll be home today during school, right mom?" The boy asked.

"Yep, I have to run some errands in a little bit here but I'll be home by noon." The mother replied as she presented the boy with a steaming cup of black coffee.

The boy took the cup from his mother and thanked her before continuing.

"Okay, well I'm going to go over the final list with Adam so if I need anything can I text you and have you lay it out for me on my bed?"

"Yeah of course, are you set on clothes and deodorant? You're camping with girls so you don't want to smell like raccoon piss and lake water the entire time."

This brought laughter to both of them as the boy rolled his eyes and confirmed that he did in fact have plenty of clean clothes and deodorant.

"Alright good, just looking out for my boy. Besides, Jfer had mentioned something to me about how you get a bit stinky when you sweat."

"That's just the essence of man." The boy said with a chuckle as he scooped a bite of scrambled eggs into his mouth.

"Hey all I'm saying is that she's a cool girl and I think you two would make a good match. And you never know, you could want some company in that four-person tent of yours." With this the mother shot a smirk in the boy's direction witch nearly made him choke on the sip of coffee he had taken.

"Jesus Christ are you suggesting that I have sex with Jfer? That's disgusting you're my mother!"

"Hey! I never said anything about sex, but the nights could get cold and sharing body heat is one of the best ways to stay warm."

"Okay you're done. No more comments from you." The boy was starting to get uncomfortable with where the conversation was going. For some reason his mother had been trying to play matchmaker for Jfer and him since the first day she had met the girl. She had even gone so far as inviting Jfer to a family dinner sometime in the near future.

The boy hadn't forgotten that night of his first trip in the park, when he had connected with Jfer both physically and emotionally. It had seemed as if Jfer was totally into him at the time. Lately though she had been treating him more and more like a good friend or a brother since he had started hanging out with the garage squad. Of course there was the sly flirting that seemed to slip into every conversation they had, but other than that there had been no progression in the connection between the two.

As the boy finished his meal he wrapped up the weekends plans with his mother.

"Alright so I'll be back home by two-thirty to shower, grab something to eat, and get ready. Adam's picking me up at four and we're heading up to his place where the rest of the group will have already set up camp for us. I'll be home by six on Tuesday and if I need anything I'll call you."

"Sounds good." Then, in a more serious tone his mother added, "and if you wouldn't mind just calling to check in with us every day. It seems crazy but your father and I will want to hear from you."

"Alright mom, I can do that. Does it matter what time I call?"

"No I suppose it doesn't, just try to catch us after dinner if you can. That'll probably be the time we're worrying the most about you."

The boy smiled and reassured his mother that she had nothing to worry about. He then rose from his seat to give the woman a hug and a goodbye, and grabbed his backpack. As the boy walked out of the house he thought about just how much he loved his parents for caring about him like they did. He knew that other members of the squad—including Jfer—weren't as lucky to have such great parents as he did. As a matter of fact most of the other kids came from either divorced households or parents that had simply given up on them. Adam was the one person that seemed to have a relatively good home life; even better than his own in some cases.

He took a long gulp of coffee before getting into the Challenger and beginning his commute to school. On the way he resisted the urge to smoke a cigarette, and instead sipped his way through the cup of coffee while listening to a new album Jfer had showed him the week before. The boy had listened through the album several times already and was starting to catch onto the lyrics.

Jfer had an interesting taste in music. It wasn't emo rock necessarily, but it was a mixture of classical rock music and poetic lyrics, interspersed with the occasional scream session. The boy wouldn't consider it his new favorite genre, but he liked the meaning behind the songs and the classical rock influences.

As he pulled into the parking lot he mentally prepared himself for the day of school and tried to suppress his growing anxiety about the camping trip. He knew that whatever was to come, would come. If he couldn't handle whatever it was, the group would just have to understand. Despite the attitude of optimism that he carried, his knees were still shaking when he got out of the car and began walking towards the campus.

Chapter 12

The boy had purposely arrived ten minutes before school started so that he could meet up with the squad in Mr. Jensen's room. The teacher had become almost a part of the group. He would offer the students tutoring during lunch or before and after school, and if they didn't need tutoring they were still welcome to hang out in the room until the bell rang so long as they didn't disrupt other students who were there for help with math.

The boy had never disclosed the details of his relationship with Mr. Jensen to the group. The fact that he and the teacher regularly talked and smoked cigarettes after school had been something he didn't want the others to know. If they found out, the boy would never hear the end of their teacher's pet insults.

In the three weeks that had gone by since Mr. Jensen showed the boy the secret garden, they had met there every day to discuss life, literature, people, and places while enjoying a cigarette. The boy was more like Mr. Jensen than he had originally thought, and the man had plenty of wisdom to offer.

When the boy first entered the room there was a silent pause while the heads of every group member turned to look at the initiate. Adam spoke up first, attempting to quell the boy's nerves.

"Looks like the fresh meat showed up for dinner guys."

The group laughed at this as the boy shot an irritated look at Adam.

"Just messing with you man, you excited?" Adam said, trying to spark the boy's spirits.

"Yeah, but can you please explain to me why you insisted on taking me up separately and only after the rest of these fucks had an hour up there to set up? I swear I step off that RV and get lit up by paintball guns or something I'll get every single one of you back."

Adam laughed at this and Frankie—one of the original four members of the squad—chimed in with "don't worry, the paintball guns don't come out until Sunday." After saying this he shot a mischievous grin around the room at the rest of the group.

The boy gave an uneasy chuckle, he could never tell when Frankie was being serious or just fucking with him.

"Don't worry, it's just the first night. The first night is when we relax and settle in. Everyone else is leaving earlier to set up, we get the VIP treatment and don't have to lift a finger. That reminds me, you have your own tent for the first night, right?"

"Alright well as long as there are no paintballs I'm fine with the VIP lifestyle. But yeah it's sitting in the trunk of my car."

"Okay cool, Maria and Nate can you two make sure to meet us at Jake's car before you head out? You have room in the trunk for another tent right?"

The boy named Nate spoke up, "yeah we can take it up don't worry about it, we'll meet you in the parking lot after school."

"Perfect, and Jake you made sure to get all the extra supplies I asked you about?"

When Adam said extra supplies the boy knew he was talking about the weed and alcohol in his third bag. While Mr. Jensen probably wouldn't have cared if they spoke openly, the group kept the more illegal aspects of the trip out of common conversation just to be safe.

"Yeah I got everything we need," the boy replied, happy to know he would be contributing something to the group. Everyone was given a list of supplies they had to bring, and while the boy's list had been the smallest, he figured that wasn't much of a complaint to have. He was secretly glad that he didn't have to drop too much money on drugs and alcohol that was to be split between eleven other people.

"Atta kid. Okay guys the bell is going to ring soon so I'll see you all here at lunch to continue going over the plan. Jake, you're not invited."

"What? Why not?" The boy asked incredulously.

"Because we're going to be planning the paintball attack on you, okay? Now just accept the fact that this weekend is not in your control, it's in ours. The less questions you ask, the easier it will be for you."

"Fair enough," the boy said, forcing himself to accept the idea of going into the trip completely blindfolded.

After Adam gave a final good luck to anybody taking a test that day, the group left the classroom and split up in the directions of their first period classes. The boy couldn't figure out whether he was more nervous or excited for the camping trip. He had built up enough trust with the members of the group already, and he knew they wouldn't do anything too savage to him. But still, he never really knew what to expect with this group of kids.

The day dragged on, and when the final bell rang the boy nearly sprinted out the door of his class. After meeting up with Adam, Nate, and Maria in the parking lot and entrusting them with his new tent, the boy set off for home to prepare and wait for Adam to pick him up.

The boy's mom laid out a dinner of steak, tater tots, and Caesar salad for the boy when he was done in the shower. The boy was nervous to the point that he didn't have much of an appetite, but he managed to force down enough food to satisfy his mother. About twenty minutes before Adam was supposed to pick the boy up, his dad came home early from work. The two went over the weekend plan again just as the boy had done with his mother that morning. Interestingly enough his father too asked the boy to call and check in at least once a day.

After a few minutes of casual conversation between the boy and his parents, there came a knock at the door.

"That must be Adam!" The boy's mom called out as she walked over to open the front door. The boy took this as his cue to go grab his bags.

While Adam distracted his parents the boy got all three bags of luggage, an air mattress, and a sleeping bag out of the house and loaded into the RV without any form of inspection from his parents. The one thing Adam was really good at was talking to parents. He could keep them focused on him long enough for the boy to slip an elephant out the side door without his parents ever noticing.

After a final goodbye to his parents, the boy followed Adam out to the RV and jumped into the passenger seat.

"Okay, so you're absolutely sure you brought everything, right?" Adam asked as he fastened his seat belt.

"Yep. Got my tooth brush, my deodorant, a couple condoms, and a metric shitload of weed and booze."

"Alright, did you bring your tampons too?"

"Oh shit I almost forgot!" The boy said as he feigned taking off his seatbelt and opening the passenger door in a rush.

"Alright well don't forget those, you'll need 'em pussy."

"Oh please, I can handle a camping trip." The boy said. He had attempted to sound smug but his voice had cracked about halfway through the statement, revealing his true nervousness in regards to the weekend.

Adam laughed and said, "We'll see about that." Before shifting the RV into gear and officially kicking off the weekend.

Chapter 13

It was a four hour drive to Adam's land, but the ride went quickly as the boys competed to see who had better taste in music, who could name the most sluts at their school in one breath, and who could spit a better freestyle rap. The two smoked joints on the way, so by the time they finally pulled into the dirt road that cut through Adam's property, they were at a good level to start off the weekend.

After cautiously driving down the bumpy dirt road for a couple hundred meters, he took a hard right into a small split in the dense pine forest. Branches from the trees whipped the RV as it brushed past them, and finally after about a minute of following the small lane through the forest, a clearing seemed to spring up out of nowhere.

The clearing was big enough for four cars to be parked in a semicircle around the back edge of trees, and there was an open space of about a hundred square yards in the center that was obviously the campground.

As the RV rolled into camp and parked just outside of the tents near a gas, water, and electricity unit, the boy realized in awe why the rest of the group had arrived earlier to set up camp. At the center of the campground was a fire pit, not the kind of cheap table top fire pits that can be found at any outdoor furnishings store. No, the fire pit was built on a base of red bricks, and surrounding the rim of the bricks flat stones had been laid by hand. The fire pit was big enough for a bonfire, but had clearly been built many years ago, as some of the rocks on top of the brick were loose and could be pulled off.

Surrounding the fire pit were four ten-foot long benches, made out of large logs that had a quarter cut out of each one to create not just a seat, but a backrest as well. Behind those were three tents, two large six-person tents and his own smaller four person tent. While it was impressive enough that the group had set up the tents already, that wasn't even the coolest part of the campsite. Between each tent was a pop-up canopy that stood over a table. Each table was set with a gas lamp in the center, a small grill and camp stove on one end, and chairs lining either side.

The group had also strung Christmas lights up between the canopies and the tents, so that even in the dark the entire campsite would be lit by the warm glow of the luminescent bulbs. Scattered around the campsite were the members of the group going about their business and putting the finishing touches on what would be their home for the next four days. Some carried bags from the cars to the tents, while others set out coolers and strung bear bags up in the trees. In the far corner of the campsite Nate and Frankie could be seen stacking firewood that they had hauled up the mountain in Nate's truck.

As the boy looked out upon the squad going about their duties, he was struck by how much they resembled an ant farm. Even better, they were like a well-oiled machine. Every person had their role, they knew what to do, and they were efficient at doing it.

Once the boy had taken a moment to absorb everything that he was seeing, Adam asked what he thought of the place.

"I think it's awesome, you guys obviously know what you're doing. This place looks incredible." The boy said, still trying to figure out how the group had managed to set everything up in just over an hour.

"Well this is our eighth time doing this so we've pretty much got it down to a science at this point," Adam said as he turned the engine off and pulled the keys from the ignition. "Come on, let's get you set up in your tent."

The boy followed Adam to the back of the RV where he had stored his bags. Before he could take them Adam began opening them and searching the contents inside. When he arrived at the second bag the boy watched as Adam pulled out every wire and electronic device he had stowed away, and placed it in a small black trash bag.

"What the fuck man? That's my stuff!" The boy said, upset by Adams intrusion into his personal belongings.

"You won't need any of it, oh and by the way give me your phone." Adam replied as he stuck his hand out expectantly in the boy's direction.

"No. You can't take my phone, what if it's an emergency and I need it?"

"Don't trip Jake, another member of the group will always be close enough to assist you. You don't need your phone."

"I have to call my parents every night around seven though, to check in."

"So you come to me and ask to borrow your phone. Listen man we all know not to use our phones up here. It's disrespectful to each other, and it's disrespectful to the trip itself. I take the initiates phones every time because they need to appreciate just being up here in nature with good friends. Once you've been through it once without a phone you won't feel the need to be on your phone the next time we go camping."

"This is ridiculous. I feel like I'm at Boy Scout camp all over again."

"Oh don't worry this is much more fun than any camping you did, girl scout. Now hand it over."

With reluctance the boy pulled his phone from his pocket and gave it to Adam.

"Good boy Jake!" Adam said exuberantly, as if he was talking to a dog.

Once the boy had laid out his bags and set up his bed in the four-person tent he took a lap around the campsite, catching up with everyone's journey and expressing his utmost amazement at how well the whole campsite turned out. Most people thanked him for the compliment, but others told him to save the gratitude for later when he would apparently "see the camp in a whole new light." While the boy wasn't sure what they meant by that, he was sure he'd find out soon.

After the sun had completely set in the horizon, and it was finally as dark as the night would get, the boy was tasked with starting the fire. With the whole group gathered around him, the boy tried to recall the skills he had learned in Boy Scouts. With no lighter fluid or artificial quick-light logs to help him, he resorted to the simplest design he knew, a small teepee of twigs with easy-to-light kindling at the center. The teepee turned out to be a smart choice, as the boy got the small fire burning within a couple minutes. After he was satisfied with the strength of the flames, he placed four logs in a larger teepee overtop of the smaller one.

Once the flames began to crawl up the logs, the boy sat back and enjoyed his piece of work. Jfer finally made it over to the campfire and sat down next to the boy on the log. The group complimented him on a good first attempt, and while some made jokes about him being an Eagle Scout he knew it was all good-natured humor. Nobody really meant to offend anyone else in the group, the jabs and sarcastic comments were just how they showed affection. They were a thick-skinned group, but at the end of the day it helped them get along well.

After a few minutes of silence and appreciation for the warmth of the fire, Adam spoke up.

"Alright guys, welcome to spring camp."

This was welcomed with cheers, whistles and a "Fuck yeah!" by Nate.

"As you all know, we have only one initiate this season, our friend Jake over here."

The group responded in unison with a monotone "hi Jake" as if they were at an AA meeting.

"Hey guys," the boy said with a casual wave.

Adam continued, "so while Jake doesn't know what's in store for him tonight, we certainly do, don't we guys?"

The menacing and mischievous laughs from the group made the boy uneasy.

"You see Jake, we like to throw the newbies straight into the melting pot up here. First night of camp; Drug Olympics!"

This was met with more cheers and celebration from the group, and the boy felt a wave of relief wash over him. No five mile run in his boxers, no eating strange food with a blindfold on, nothing like what he had been expecting from the group.

"Sounds good, what do we start with?" The boy said, confident that he would be able to handle himself through whatever challenges Adam sent his way.

The drug Olympics started with each member taking a tab of acid and popping an Ecstasy pill. Adam then pulled out a giant bamboo pipe that looked like something a wizard or a Rastafarian would smoke out of. By the time the bowl was packed there had to have been at least an eighth loaded.

"Puff, puff, pass the peace pipe please. To symbolize the unity and friendship that brought us all here tonight." Adam said as he dipped one end of the pipe into the fringes of the flame and pulled on the other end.

"He takes this way too seriously," the boy whispered into Jfers ear.

"We know, he thinks he's our spiritual leader or some shit. We let him believe that because it's funny to see how into-character he gets." Jfer whispered back with a muffled laugh.

As the peace pipe was passed around over the next thirty minutes the clouds that had previously been blocking the moon were drawn away like curtains. The moon wasn't full, but it was certainly close to it and shed plenty of light down on the clearing where the campsite was. The ground was lit up by the silvery-blue light of the moon and everywhere but the dense tree line was illuminated by its glow.

As each member of the group slowly began to trip, the boy felt the familiar presence of a trip coming towards him. He wasn't feeling the effects just yet, but he knew they were coming. The boy lost track of time once the trip began, but it didn't really matter to him. Without the notion of time the boy wouldn't be thinking about how much longer he'd be tripping for, or when the effects would start to wear off. He could simply enjoy the company of his new friends, and absorb the beauty of the forest around him.

After what seemed like an hour or two Adam restarted the rotation of the peace pipe. With twelve people sitting around a campfire it was impossible to hold one conversation, so most people chatted with those closest to them. The boy was asking Jfer about the first camping trip the group went on when Adam suddenly rose from his seat and announced it was time for the first night hike.

The first night hike was used to get everyone's bearings set on where they were on the property, and how to always find their way back to camp from anywhere on the property. It started with a walk around the perimeter which proved to take much longer than the boy had expected. At one point the group came upon a stream that crossed over the far eastern perimeter. Adam explained that if one was ever lost they need only to follow the perimeter fence to the creek. The hiker could then follow the creek for a couple minutes until the light of the campground was visible.

After explaining this to the group Adam led them up the creek back to the campground. The property was fairly simple to navigate, it was a square plot of land fenced in on all sides by barbed wire. When the boy mentioned how surprised he was by the simple layout of the property Jfer gave him a look like he should've expected that.

"Well it's kind of just a big playground for hippy adults and stupid teenagers to experiment with drugs when you think about it. I heard Adam's parents did Peyote up here during their honeymoon."

"Are you serious? God his parents are nuts," the boy replied in astonishment. Even after spending a substantial amount of time with the King family, Mr. and Mrs. King never ceased to amaze the boy. They had no limits, no points where they would draw the line. If they wanted to do something, they'd do it one way or another. That kind of devil-may-care attitude was something the boy envied about all three members of the King family.

When the group finally arrived back at camp from the first night hike, Adam unveiled the next drug to the group; Cocaine. Each person was to rail two lines, one to help pick up the intensity of the trip, and one to help keep them awake to experience it. Any more than two of the small powdery lines could result in an abnormal heartbeat and health problems, so Adam made it very clear that nobody was to take more than two lines.

This was the boy's first encounter with the white lady, and he wasn't sure what to expect. He was hesitant to put the rolled up dollar bill to his nose, but after seeing the look on everyone else's face after their two lines, he made a "why the fuck not?" call in his head and took the two lines.

After the jitters finally calmed down the boy felt the effects of all three drugs in his system at once. It was a lot to take in, so he leaned back against the log and stared up at the sky while snapping his wrist with the rubber band that he still had from his first trip. As he was staring up into the night sky he began to notice just how many more stars could be seen from up in the mountains compared to back at home. With no light pollution from any major cities, and an elevation of approximately six thousand feet, the sky was bursting with stars that danced and formed patterns in front of the boy's eyes.

After a while the group began to break off into groups, some opting to play beer pong, others choosing to make s'mores, and the rest either playing poker or taking a hike with a buddy. The boy didn't know what he wanted to do, but Jfer pulled him along on a hike with two other members of the squad; Eric and Mackenzie.

As they walked the boy gained more information on two of the squad members he hadn't spent very much time with previously. He learned that Eric and Mackenzie had been dating for a year before they met Nate and joined the group. They were the only official couple in the group, since Nate and Maria were more like fuckbuddies than anything serious.

As the group of four began to march up the hill in the northeastern corner of the King's property, conversation ceased in order to conserve oxygen. Hiking at such high altitudes while on so many drugs was not a safe idea to begin with, but in order to make it through it seemed to the boy that one must simply focus on conserving energy the right way.

By the time they reached the top of the hill the morning sun was starting to leak onto the canvas that was the blue night sky. As the group sat and watched the sky went from deep navy blue, to a lighter shade, and then slowly but surely bright yellow and orange began to splash over the horizon. The sun's rising signaled the hibernation of the teens, so after watching the sun fully pull itself over the horizon line, the group made their way back to camp. By the time they arrived back the drugs had worn off and they were all ready for bed. The boy wasn't allowed to sleep in the squad tent until the night ahead, so he retired alone to his four-person tent and began to prepare himself for bed. Just as he was stripping out of his jeans to put on gym shorts, a quick zipping notified him that somebody was entering the tent.

As the boy quickly pulled up the gym shorts he turned to see Jfer stepping into the tent, zipping the doorway closed behind her.

"No way in hell I'm sleeping in that tent with five other people. Too much body heat and heavy snoring." Jfer said as she pushed her hair from out of her face.

"Well feel free to barge right in, why don't you?" The boy replied sarcastically.

"You're going to tell me you don't want me in here with you?" Jfer said with a smug look on her face. She knew the boy was happy she had decided to join him. This was the first chance she had given him since the incident with Amanda at the party. Jfer knew the boy would pounce on it.

"No, no I don't think I will. As a matter of fact, it's good to have you, welcome to my trap-tent." The boy said with a stupid grin on his face.

"You are retarded." Jfer replied before stripping down to nothing but her panties and crawling into the boy's sleeping bag.

"Look at you making yourself comfortable in my bed." The boy said with mock irritation.

"Well I'm sorry, I just figured it looked big enough for two." Jfer replied in a dreamy overdramatic voice.

The boy stood there for a moment, trying to figure out what Jfer's play was. After struggling to find a reasonable solution he decided not to label the naked girl in his sleeping bag a problem, but a very, very, good thing. He slipped out of his gym shorts and joined the girl inside the sleeping bag. It had only been the first night of the campout, and the boy was enjoying himself already. After hooking up for a short period of time, both Jfer and the boy decided it would be best to get some sleep and try to wake up before night fell. The last thought that raced through the boy's head as he lay next to Jfer was that her hair smelled like Lavender.

Chapter 14

The boy awoke to a most pleasant surprise. Jfer had obviously woken up before him, and was enjoying her breakfast in bed. More specifically, Jfer was enjoying the boy as breakfast in bed. For a moment he thought he was dreaming, but as the girl looked up at him with her brilliant bright eyes, he snapped into reality all too soon. Luckily Jfer wasn't the type to make a mess so after swallowing she pushed herself up and gave the boy a kiss on the cheek.

"Morning," she said with a smile before pulling the boy's boxers back up to his hips.

"That was easily the most beautiful thing I've ever woken up to." The boy said, a smile playing at the ends of his mouth.

"What, me sucking your dick?" Jfer said with a look of pride.

"No, well yes, but no." The boy could see that Jfer wasn't understanding what he was getting at. "Just waking up to you. I mean don't get me wrong that whole surprise alarm clock thing you did was pretty fucking astounding. I'm not complaining, it's just that I've always wanted to wake up to a beautiful girl next to me. You-"

"Jake just shut up please. For one second. You're so much cuter when you aren't trying to be some hopeless romantic."

"Uhm, okay. I guess?" The boy was puzzled by the girl. Jfer was like a maze. Every wrong turn would result in a dead end. She wasn't shy about letting him know that either, she could send him straight back to the start of the maze at any time.

"Good, now here's the deal," Jfer said as she straddled the boy's waist and leaned her weight forward onto her hands, pinning the boy down. "I'm staying in this tent at night with you, and you're staying in this tent at night with me, for the rest of the weekend. Deal?"

"And what happens if I make it through all three nights without getting sick of you?" The boy asked as he raised one eyebrow in a challenging manner.

"Good luck to you then bud, because you probably will have fallen in love by the end of it." Jfer said before leaning down to kiss the boy. As she pulled away from him she bit the edge of his lip and pulled hard. It hurt, but the look she gave him afterwards made the pain vanish almost immediately. Jfer picked herself up off the boy and began to get dressed.

The boy was still not quite sure what he had done right with Jfer, but he couldn't complain considering the treatment she was giving him. After standing up and getting dressed himself, the boy followed Jfer out of the tent and into the afternoon sun.

"How late did we sleep?" The boy asked as the two walked towards one of the tables with a grill set up.

"It's one-thirty." Jfer replied emotionlessly.

"What the hell, we slept until one-thirty? Jesus Christ when did we finally go to sleep?" The boy asked in shock.

"I want to say it was around five, maybe a half after you-couldn't-get-it-up o'clock." The girl replied as she looked back with a smirk.

"Hey." The boy stopped and looked at her with more than a little embarrassment. "It's not my fault you tried to kill me with a Drug Olympics last night."

The girl only smiled as she continued towards the breakfast table. Adam was hard at work cooking up breakfast for lunch, and as the boy approached the table he caught the unmistakable aroma of sizzling bacon.

"Morning kids, how was last night?" Adam asked with a grin. He looked something like a model out of a *Great Outdoors* catalog. He was wearing sweatpants and slippers, a hoodie with a beanie on, and dark sunglasses to ease the sunlight's effect on his hungover head. The funniest part of the entire outfit was the beer in one hand and the spatula he held in his other.

"Good, cold." Jfer replied as she passed a paper plate to Adam. "Bacon and two pancakes please."

"Yeah it was pretty cold last night, you almost gutted me a couple times with those diamond-cutters." The boy said as he shot an almost-wink in the direction of Jfer.

"Well at least something in that tent was hard last night." Jfer replied with an icy look.

With no comeback for the girl the boy simply laughed and passed Adam a plate, asking for the works and a beer.

After the food had been washed down with cold frothy ale and a cigarette, the trio attempted to piece the night together. As they each retold parts of the story that they remembered more and more of the squad filed into place for breakfast. Each person had their own memories of the night. Their own story to tell.

The boy found it interesting that despite twelve people equally being fucked up, they all recalled bits and pieces of the same story, the same general adventure that the night had been. The more he thought about it the more he felt in-touch with the people around him. They all knew how trashed they had been the night before, but it didn't seem to matter to any of them. There was no embarrassment because there were no lies. Every single person was genuinely honest with what parts of the night they remembered. While some memories were more accurate than others, everyone remembered their own separate reality of the night before. Every reality seemed to follow the same story arc.

It was almost like dreaming, the boy thought. Everybody had their own separate and individual dreams, but the dreams led everyone to the same place. Jfer broke the boy from his spell by suggesting a hike. Since he had nothing better to do than get inebriated and go hiking, he figured Jfer would be a fun companion to have along for the journey. After rolling a couple joints for the trip the two set off alone in the direction of one of the peaks overlooking the mountain.

Jfer had told the boy it would be about a mile and a half hike, so when they had been walking continuously with no elevation gain for over an hour, the two finally accepted that they were lost. Luckily they had managed to find their way towards a more residential area of the mountain, so they stopped to sit on the side of a trail.

Behind them was densely forested land, in front of them stood two log cabins which obviously belonged to seasonal owners who wouldn't return until the weather did in some extreme or another. Jfer explained to the boy how most of the residents only came up to their cabins when it was too hot back home or not snowy enough for their holiday tastes.

"Funny how those who are rich enough can literally determine their own environment." The boy brought up after the two had smoked their second joint.

"Well yeah, I mean that's how it's supposed to be you know? The privileged get the best opportunities." Jfer replied as she lay back into the pine needles that covered the forest floor.

"No. No. That's not how it's supposed to be. We're all made of the same shit. We all crawled our way out of the same dirt. Why the hell do some get to choose their comfort zone while others are stuck in the same dirt we came from?" The boy was getting more and more heated by the topic the more he thought it over.

"Wow. Somebody's feeling a little rant-y this morning." Jfer said as she sat back up and put her arm around the boy.

"Afternoon, thanks to you." The boy replied. "And hear me out. Whoever the owner of this castle-in-the-woods is can clearly afford a very expensive second and maybe third home for himself and his family. Why can't he be a decent fucking person and put that money to better use? Send it to Africa or some shit so that he can build twenty houses for the price of his one up here. I mean it's not too crazy of a concept is it?" The boy asked as he turned to look at the girl.

"Well that's a very humanitarian thought. I like that. Unfortunately though, the guy who owns this house is probably so caught up in his own world of executive meetings, six-figure salary checks, and slutty secretaries that the kids in Africa aren't even a part of his reality anymore. Think about it. When you hear about the starving and homeless people in the world you hear about it on the news, you see it on TV. Everyone seems to have this fucked up moral compass that tells them there is a totally different reality and dimension that is contained inside a tiny box in front of them. Once they walk away from the box they have the opportunity to accept the true reality of everything they see on TV and in their own life, or accept the comfort of their own reality."

"That's a pretty fucked up theory you have of mankind, you know that JFer?"

"Is it that far from the truth?"

The boy knew it was the truth, or at least close to it, but instead of giving her the satisfaction of being right he pulled a cigarette out, put it to his lips, and lit it.

"You can help stop forest fires." Jfer said as she pulled the stoag from his fingers and put it to her own lips.

"So do you ever have your own pack of cigs or are you just a constant mooch?"

"I like sharing cigarettes. It adds to the community aspect of them."

"How so?"

"Well when you smoke a cigarette with another person, they do the talking while you smoke your cigarette, and vice versa. Instead of creating that pause when both of you are talking or smoking, if you pass the cigarette throughout conversation it opens windows to talk and windows to listen."

"You have a reason for everything, don't you?"

Jfer put the cigarette to the boy's lips in response.

"Shh. It's your turn to smoke now."

Chapter 15

The weekend continued with as much youthful rebellion and as many felonies as the first night. Saturday afternoon there was a beer pong tournament, but before starting the tournament every member of the group had to smoke a gram of weed each. The boy got another taste of stoner culture and etiquette. For instance, when smoking in a group of more than three people, it was inappropriate to call Marco and Polo. Instead "deuces" and "trips" were called to determine rotation.

At some point during the weekend the boy found a minute to himself while he was relieving himself just past the tree-line. He began to think how odd it was that he had found a group of individuals with whom he shared a mutual connection. The boy had friends. Not just friends, he had a squad. The feelings he had towards all of them were foreign, alien, and weird. He had never cared much about his peer groups—or if they cared about him— but now he genuinely cared about these kids. It all worried the boy. He knew that in a few short months they'd be going their separate ways.

The boy had received a letter in the days leading up to the camping trip that had decided the path of his future. The boy had been accepted to Michigan State, and would be attending the school in August. He hadn't told anyone yet, as most of the kids were to be attending junior colleges and living with their parents still. The boy had considered the junior college route already, but decided as much as he loved his parents, it was time for him to get out and be on his own. Even if it meant moving to cold-as-shit Michigan.

It seemed like the boy was being cheated. He had finally met a solid friend group but would be taken away from them so quickly due to the pressing demands of his future. He had decided that instead of moping and feeling sorry for himself he would soak in every experience that he could while still with the squad. This camping trip was just the first of their planned adventures together. They were going to Adam's beach house the weekend after graduation, and then two weeks later they'd be road tripping to Las Vegas for a week long music festival.

As he zipped up his jeans and trudged back into camp, a smile came to his face. Jfer was sitting at one of the tables reading *Zen and the Art of Motorcycle Maintenance*. She had a stupid look on her face, with her eyes glued to the pages but her face making strange expressions in reaction to whatever she was reading. The boy wasn't sure what attracted him most about Jfer. Perhaps it was the fact that she was imperfect, and yet was totally comfortable with all of her imperfections. The girl never once took shit from anybody, and while on the outside it made her seem like a bitch, the boy and everyone else in the squad knew that it was really because she took shit from her mother every single day and had gained a thick skin from the woman.

Maybe it was because she was gorgeous. As he came closer Jfer looked up from her book and flashed a smile at the boy. As she did her eyes caught the sun in just a way that made them glisten and gleam for a second. There was something about her eyes that always intrigued the boy. Behind the glimmer of hope that appeared in the right light, there was a sadness that could be seen. Sometimes if she drank too much or smoked too much the sadness would come out verbally in the form of tragic and depressing thoughts. Thoughts of hopelessness and apathy. Jfer had brought these thoughts to the group several times in just the short span of time that the boy had been with them, so he assumed they had been a normal occurrence even before he had come into the group.

"She's depressed," the boy reminded himself. He had seen the pills the girl had to take in the morning and at night. Even if he hadn't it was pretty easy to deduce through her thoughts sometimes. The thing about her though was that most of the time she was optimistic, happy, and outgoing. Jfer had her imperfections, and she knew that, but every day it seemed as if she strived to move past them.

"Hey you." Jfer said softly as the boy sat down next to her at the table.

"Hey, so I noticed a couple bumps down there when I was peeing, you wouldn't happen to know anything about that would you?" The boy asked with a sly grin.

"Oh shut up, it was probably Amanda that gave those to you." Jfer replied with a laugh.

"No because I used a condom with Amanda and I didn't with you." The boy returned sarcastically.

"What?!" The girl sat up and grabbed the boys arm.

"Surprise it's going to be a boy!" He said with a smile as he was bombarded with blows from the girl.

"I'm just fucking with you calm down!" He let out between laughs and hits to the head.

"I hate you." Jfer said before kissing him on the cheek and picking up her book again.

"You love me, I know." The boy said before lying down on the bench and resting his head on the girls lap. He had a whole new perspective of her face from down there, and she was still startlingly beautiful even upside down.

"What are you looking at?" Jfer said with a smile.

"Well I'm trying to look at your beautiful face but your boobs are like mountains blocking a sunrise."

"Awww that is the sweetest thing anybody's ever said to me." The girl exclaimed with mock sincerity.

"Really?" The boy asked, not catching her sarcasm.

"No asshole, stop staring at my boobs." She replied shortly.

"Fine." The boy stated as he turned his head towards her stomach.

In a cooing voice the boy began to talk to the hypothetical child in Jfer's womb.

"Hey little guy. I'm daddy, nice to meet you. You're inside mommy's tummy right now but soon you're going to be out in this big world with us, and you'll get to see mommy's beautiful face and drink from her perfect titties. I'm kind of jealous of you in a way you know."

"JAKE! FOR FUCK'S SAKE." Jfer exclaimed before the boy leaned up and pulled her into a kiss. They held the kiss for a couple seconds before Jfer pulled away.

"Oh... Okay," the girl said in a whisper.

"I love you too." The boy replied softly before resting his head back down on her lap and closing his eyes.

The two didn't know it yet, but this would be the start of a blossoming relationship. One that would change both individuals forever. The boy would look back on this day and wonder what compelled him to say those three words. He had only known Jfer for a short period of time, yet he had made a connection with her unlike any other connection he'd had before.

That night around the campfire the boy revealed to the others that he'd be leaving for Michigan at the end of the summer. In general the group was happy for him. There was also the sobering realization that their newest friend would also be gone the soonest, but with such good vibes it wasn't a sad realization, it was accepted just as much as every other person's future was; inevitable.

Jfer took the news better than the boy had thought she would. Instead of freaking out about him moving across the country like he thought she would, the girl had been very supportive of his decision, considering the fact that she would be moving two hours away for college in San Diego.

By the end of the camping trip the boy was basking in the glory of his new-found friendship. He had survived the substance hazing that had lasted three days and nights. The group respected him, and he was treated like an equal.

:::::

As the weeks went by the boy became more and more attached with his newfound friend group. The major change in his life though would turn out to be his girlfriend. As the school year came to a close and graduation approached, it was time for Jfer to meet the boy's parents officially as his girlfriend.

It was a warm spring day, and a breeze was passing through the secret garden, causing pollen to float off the freshly-bloomed flowers and swirl around in the air. The boy and girl were sitting on top of the same table Mr. Jensen had showed the boy months ago. This had become a regular occurrence for them, and they could be found in the same spot every day during lunch or between classes.

As they sat there joking about Adam's newest boy-toy and the impending freedom that graduation would bring, the two were interrupted by someone clearing their throat as they walked into the garden.

"What's up Mr. J?" The boy asked as he looked up to see the teacher strolling towards the table, a lit cigarette already between his lips.

"Not much Mr. Rivera, how are you? Jennifer?" The man said with a nod in the girls direction.

"Pretty good," the two answered in unison. Jfer shot the boy an annoyed look before laughing the synchrony off.

"Yeah? Well it sounds like you two are in each other's heads now. Isn't that cute." Mr. Jensen responded in a mocking tone.

"Oh don't worry, it annoys us too sometimes." Jfer said before turning to the boy.

"Stop copying me." They said in unison again.

"Okay that's enough. I'm about to write you both up for being that obnoxious new couple." Mr. Jensen proclaimed before rolling his eyes and taking a seat on the table next to the boy. After a moment of quietly dragging on their cigarettes the boy spoke up.

"So JFer's meeting my parents tonight."

"Ahh, well good luck Jennifer. I've been in parent-teacher conferences with those two. They're batshit crazy." The teacher said with a cocked eyebrow.

"Oh come on you're not helping. She's already a nervous wreck about it." The boy said as he wrapped his arm around his girlfriend.

"Am not" Jfer started. "It's just the first impression is a really big deal. You know?" She finished resentfully.

"I'm just messing with you kiddo, you'll be fine. The Riveras are nice people. Just make sure not to feed them after midnight. Things get a little wacky." With this the teacher shot a wink at the girl and chuckled before taking another drag of his cigarette.

"You owe us both extra credit for that one. These ARE my parents that we're talking about after all." The boy said with a smile. "The only person that can talk shit on my parents is me."

"How honorable of you Jake, I'm sure your family would be proud." Mr. Jensen responded.

"No, but seriously Jfer." The boy continued as he turned to the girl next to him. "My mom throws things sometimes. Just be careful what you say about the Green River incident of eighty-seven."

Jfer immediately reeled in shock. "Wait what?! You never mentioned any incident about a river! How am I supposed to know what to say?" The girl's eyes were wide with fear.

"It's a little rite of passage for my family. You'll do fine." The boy replied coolly.

Mr. Jensen laughed at this and the boy expressed his sincerest apologies to the girl for joking during such a serious conversation. His sorry was met with a sarcastic "it's fine" before Jfer called him an obscenity even he hadn't heard before.

As the three continued talking and smoking their cigarettes the boy realized how much had changed since that first night with Jfer and Adam. He not only had friends that he shared mutual respect with, but he had a girlfriend who adored him, a teacher which respected him, and parents which suspected nothing. This was a peak for the boy. And while he didn't know it yet, there amongst the blooming flowers and crawling critters of the garden was a fat lady singing a mournful tune.

The lunch bell signaled all three to ash their cigarettes and make their way to class. After parting ways with Jfer and finalizing their plans for the evening, the boy followed Mr. Jensen to his classroom for Math. Mr. Jensen had pushed the students to finish the book at break-neck speed in order to grant them three weeks of finals prep. The first week of finals preparation had been taken as a complete joke though, considering nearly every student in the class was a disastrous procrastinator.

The bell soon rang again, sending the underclassmen to their final period and releasing the upperclassmen for the day. By the time the bell had rung the boy was already turning up his street. Mr. Jensen had let the boy out early as a gift before his possibly miserable night ahead. As the boy rolled up the street and approached the driveway he noticed a strange car in his spot. He had never seen this car before, and he didn't think his mom was having someone over before his girlfriend arrived in a few hours. Needless to say the boy was a little concerned as he stepped out of the car and made his way up to the driveway. Just to play it safe the boy went through the back door. He didn't want to smell like cigarettes, weed, and sweat if he walked in on his aunt from out of town in his kitchen.

But as the boy made his way to his bedroom to reinforce his layer of deodorant and flush the redness out of his eyes, he heard a noise that made his heart sink. He had heard the noise before. This wasn't the same sound of sex that he knew through his girlfriend. These were sex noises straight off of Pornhub. Over-the-top, unnecessarily loud, and grotesque. The boy was in such shock he said the only thing that came to mind.

"Mom, I'm home!" The boy shouted down the hall before immediately retreating behind the closed door of his room. As he tried to shake the horrible sounds out of his head something struck him like a lightning bolt. His father's car wasn't in the driveway. His mother's was on the street like it usually was, but his father's car was not in the driveway. No- there had been a different, alien car in his driveway.

The boy stopped in his tracks as the full force of what was happening hit him square in the jaw. His mother was cheating. She was in the bedroom with another man cheating on his father. It took the boy less than three seconds to furiously tear out of his room and bolt past his mother who was standing in the front doorway with her arms outstretched. The woman had a stupid look on her face as if she wasn't sure whether to stop him or break down in tears. The boy caught up to the man on the driveway and dragged him by the collar of his shirt onto the front lawn.

The man was bigger than the boy, but had clearly never been thrown into a situation like this. The car was a luxurious sedan, and the designer glasses the boy smashed with the first blow were going to cost him a month's allowance and car privileges. None of that mattered to the boy. All that mattered to him in that moment as he stood over the man was one thing. He wanted to hurt this man as much as the man was about to hurt his family. After another smashing punch to the jaw. The boy pinned the man by his neck and said in the scariest tone he could muster, "Who the fuck are you, and what the fuck is going to happen if I see you on my property or near my mother again?"

"My name is Kyle Favarti." The man let out between tears. "I don't know. I don't know!"

"Stay away from my family Kyle!" The boy yelled as he dug his forearm into the man's throat. After seeing his eyes bulge in fear the boy pulled off of him. Kyle had never been in a fight before. He had never even taken a punch it seemed like. It was wrong of the boy to go all street fighter on the poor guy. As Kyle skittered back into his car and drove off the boy slowly reached into his pocket and pulled the keys from the very bottom. Only then did he turn and finally notice his mother standing in the doorway sobbing. She had nothing on but a robe and was covering her mouth with one hand while shaking her head at the boy.

"H-honey. I-I sw-swear it only happened once. I'm sorry. I fucked up. I fucked up!" The woman let all of this out between tears and gasps for breath. The boy could hardly look at her. The woman he had loved and idolized all his life, his caretaker, his god-damned mother, had cheated on his hard-working father with a pathetic man who threw around money to impress people.

"You will tell Dad. When you do, I'll come home." Was all he could muster up before calmly walking to his car and driving off, leaving his mother crying in the front .

Chapter 16

Fifteen miles per hour. Thirty, then sixty, then eighty. By the time the boy had merged onto the freeway his Challenger was pushing one hundred miles per hour. He was so distracted by the thoughts swirling through his brain that he didn't notice the cop two cars behind him. How could his mother do this to his father? After everything the man had provided for her, this was how she repaid him. He couldn't stand the thought of what he had walked in on, but the awful noises couldn't be cleared from his head no matter how loud his music was.

It wasn't until the police car caught up beside the Challenger with its lights flashing that the boy finally realized he had passed one hundred and twenty miles per hour. He slowed down immediately and pulled over towards the shoulder, finally slowing down to a complete stop.

"Just my fucking luck," the boy said aloud as he reached into his glove box and pulled out the vehicle registration card. Moments later the cop's head poked through the driver's side window.

"Son, just what the hell do you think you're doing?" The officer started.

"I'm sorry sir I had a family emergency. I wasn't thinking straight." The boy muttered back as he looked down at his lap in disappointment. He had never been given a speeding ticket, and he didn't plan on getting one today. Hopefully the sympathy card would play out.

"What kind of family emergency requires you to break a hundred miles an hour on a busy freeway?" The cop asked with a touch of sarcasm.

"Well to be completely honest sir I walked in on my mom cheating on my dad. I had to get away from that situation, and I didn't keep an eye on my speed. Again, I'm really sorry and I'll be more cautious."

The cop seemed interested in this new information, so he took the boy's license and walked back to his car, telling the boy not to move from where he had stopped. Of course there was a split second where the boy was tempted to speed off down the freeway, but he imagined he wouldn't get too far and attempting to evade police would only make his day worse.

The cop returned bearing news that the boy's mother had called 911 in a panic and requested that her son be brought home immediately. Since the boy was still seventeen for another month, the cop had to bring him home to his mother. Luckily, the officer seemed to feel some sort of sympathy for the boy, and allowed him to drive his own car home safely while the cop followed him.

As the officer reached forward to return the boy's license, his name tag caught a gleam of afternoon sunlight. "Officer Jensen" The nametag read, but the boy didn't think much of it at the time. He was more focused on getting out of his speeding ticket and what troubles awaited him back home.

With the officer following close behind, the boy took the five minute drive home as slowly as he could. It didn't matter what his mother said upon his return, the boy made up his mind that she was to be excommunicated. He just hoped his father and sister would feel the same.

As the boy pulled back up the street Kyle's car was nowhere to be seen. Probably a good thing considering it would take more than one police officer to restrain the boy if he ever saw the man again. The boy's mother answered the door with wide eyes. Luckily she had found time to replace her post-affair robe with more modest clothing.

"Hello officer, thank you for bringing Jake home." She began. "I don't know what he told you but I can assure you that your services are no longer required. Right Jake?" She said as she turned a prompting eye in the boy's direction. The boy said nothing in return so after an awkward pause the officer spoke up.

"Well sorry Mrs.-"

"Ms." The boy cut the officer off.

"Rivera." The officer said with a disdainful look towards the boy. "I have to ask just a few simple questions to make sure everything around here is cool before I leave. Can't return a minor to a house that could be potentially unstable and unsafe."

His mother had a worried look in her eye. "Of course, of course, I'm sorry. What's the first question?"

"Ma'am, this could take a few minutes, do you mind if I come inside?" The officer asked suspiciously.

"Certainly." The woman responded coldly before opening the door and leading the officer inside. Once they reached the kitchen the woman offered the man a seat at the dinner table, before bringing him a glass of water and sitting across from him. The boy took a seat in the middle of the table, mirrored on either side by his mother and the police officer. He instantly regretted choosing the seat. It made him the focus point for the two others at the table.

The officer withdrew a pen and notepad from inside his jacket and began taking down notes. After several moments of silence he looked up.

"So Mrs. Rivera what was the reason for your call at three-o-nine this afternoon?"

"Well my son had taken the family car without my permission. I wanted him back home safe so I called 911." The woman responded in a calm tone.

"Mhm." The officer murmured as he jotted the statement down on his notepad.

"And why did you take the car without your Mother's permission Jake?" He asked in a more gentle tone, turning his attention to the boy.

"I walked in on my mother cheating on my father with another man. I didn't want to explode, so I ran." The boy knew this wasn't the entire truth, his assault on Kyle could be seen as a minor "explosion," but the officer didn't have to know about it.

"Mrs. Rivera, is this true?" The officer asked accusingly.

"What? Jake I would never! How could you even think of saying something like that?" His mother's false shock seemed to catch the officer off guard, but the boy could see straight through her lies. How dare she call him a liar when the bitch had cheated on his father and called the cops on him? The officer shot the boy a look of frustration.

"Jake, what do you have to say for yourself?" The officer inquired.

"I. I don't know, maybe I overreacted and what I thought I heard was nothing." The boy said as he resigned himself to taking the loss. It was his mother's word against his, and he knew that no cop would believe the word of a spoiled minor over that of his parents.

"Alright. Well you two clearly need to have a discussion. Ma'am do you mind if I speak to Jake alone for a moment?" The officer asked as he stood up from the table.

"No sir, of course not." She replied between tight lips.

The boy stood and followed the officer out the front door, where the officer stopped and turned to face him.

"Alright son when's your birthday?" The cop started. The boy thought it odd that the policeman was calling him 'son' when he wasn't much older than the boy. The man only appeared to be in his mid-thirties. As the boy looked at the officer he noticed a striking resemblance to his teacher Mr. Jensen. The image of the name tag on his shirt flashed before the boy again.

The boy completely disregarded the man's question and instead pushed one of his own on the officer. "Hey, you don't happen to have a brother named Alex do you?"

"What?" The Officer seemed perplexed by the boy's response. "Yes but that's a weird fucking question kid you're making me uncomfortable. You're not going to come after my family are you?"

With this the boy cracked a smile, the cop was like Mr. Jensen 2.0.

"When do you turn eighteen?" The cop asked again, clearly antagonized by the boy's grin.

"I turn eighteen in a couple weeks, and your brother is my math teacher." The boy admitted in an attempt to put the officer at ease.

"Alright then, and are you moving out after graduation?" The officer asked in a more professional tone.

"Yeah I'll be going to Michigan State in August." The boy replied trying to match the officer's attitude and tone.

"Some advice. Stay here. Don't go taking the car your father bought for you out whenever the hell you please just because mommy and daddy might be having some issues."

The boy rolled his eyes in annoyance. A speech. He was getting a god-damned lecture from this cop instead of a ticket. Perfect.

"When you turn eighteen, have fun and ball out before you leave for college. But for now, play the game by the rules. You're still a minor. Remember that."

The officer made a good point. Once the boy turned eighteen he would legally be an adult and his parents would have no power over him. He could survive a few more months in the house without incident. Of course his home life would never be the same again. A fact he would have to come to terms with over the next couple weeks.

"Yes sir, I'll play it safe don't worry." The boy responded.

"And as for the speeding ticket. I think you have enough to worry about besides a court fine."

"Thank you officer, and thank you for not stressing my mom out anymore with the questions. This is the most freaked out I've ever seen her before. The thing is, I don't even know how to calm her down, or if I should. Shit I don't even know if I can speak to her right now." The boy said as he looked down at his feet.

"No problem kid, just take it one step at a time. You have a good night now, and don't make me pick you up again speeding down the freeway." The officer said this with a sincere smile and made his way back towards his car. Before he stepped into the driver's seat he turned one last time towards the boy.

"Oh, and tell my brother Alex he's a pusscake." The man added with a chuckle.

The boy cracked a smile and waved goodbye to the officer before walking back towards the house. He had no idea what was waiting for him inside, and he had no idea how he was supposed to react to it, but he knew he couldn't run from the steaming pile of shit that his mother had left

Chapter 17

The boy entered the kitchen to find his mother hunched over the kitchen sink, crying. She seemed to sense the boys' entry, because she pulled herself together and wiped her eyes before turning to face him.

"Before you waste your time, there is nothing you can say that will make this situation any better." The boy said sharply as he stared the woman down.

"I understand that." His mother replied with a sniffle. "But I think we've both had a very stressful afternoon." As she said this the boy noticed a mischievous smirk play across her face. He knew this would be the one chance for his mother to pull out the power play, or make her attempt to bribe or blackmail him. However, he was not prepared for what she said next.

"We should smoke some weed." The woman added with an attempt at a smile. "And don't ask me how I know you smoke. I'm your mother for Christ's sake. I'll meet you in the backyard." With this the woman took her leave to smoke a cigarette by the pool.

That was it. The boy's mother knew he smoked the reefer, the devil's lettuce, dope, ganja, weed, grass, whatever the fuck you wanted to call it. She knew, and she was going to let him off without punishment, that was her power play. The boy wasn't opposed to the idea of his mother turning a blind eye to his activities, so he figured it was best to at least meet his mother outside and see what she had to say for herself.

Not knowing if she was serious about the weed or not the boy decided to play it safe and only grab a small amount that he could easily say was all he had. He decided on grabbing a pre-rolled from his room and went to meet with his mother outside. The boy sat opposite the woman around the small fire pit. He couldn't look at her so instead looked down and sparked the joint.

"Did you roll that?" His mother asked.

"No, my friend got it from a clinic, they roll them for you there." He said between puffs on the joint.

"Oh so you know someone with a medical marijuana card?" His mother asked in an accusatory tone.

"Yeah mom everybody around here gets one when they turn Eighteen. Even if they don't smoke kids go to clinics, pick up weed, and then sell it to other kids who don't have medcards yet." The boy said before passing the joint over the table to the woman, testing to see how far she was willing to take this bribe.

"How easy is it to get a medcard?" His mother asked, poorly concealing her interest as she pinched the joint in her fingers and pulled it out of the boy's. Her first hit was followed by a coughing attack, in which the boy was worried if the woman was even breathing. It brought a small sense of relief when she took her second hit and stopped coughing all together.

"Sorry" his mother said with a giggle. "It's been twenty-seven years since I last smoked this shit." After taking another hit she repeated her question.

"Oh yeah, the process of getting a medical marijuana prescription is a joke. I can tell them I have anxiety and they'll write me a prescription no questions asked."

His mother seemed intrigued by the idea. "Do you plan on getting your medcard when you turn eighteen?" She asked with a smirk before passing the joint back.

"Perhaps." The boy responded. He wasn't sure how his mom would react to the idea of him getting a medcard, especially since he was still not sure how she felt about smoking in the first place. It didn't seem like she had a problem with it. She was sharing the joint with him after all.

"How long have you known that I smoke weed? What was it that gave me away?" He asked in return.

"Well you see hon, a long time ago I was a bit of a Hippie myself. My Uncle grew pot in his backyard so during family reunions my cousins and I would stay at Uncle Jerry's and smoke weed all night. I first noticed the smell in your room this past summer. I'd come in to wake you up in the morning and it would occasionally smell like weed. Then finally one night you left your piece out on your desk. I walked in and saw it there, but for your own sake I hid it in your desk before waking you up. Oh and then it was the car! Jake I don't know why you think it's a good idea to smoke in there with just the windows rolled down. Why do you think I've always supplied you with air fresheners? I'm your mother and an ex-stoner. I pick up on these things, but I trust you and I believe that if you're experimenting with weed then that's a natural thing for a senior in high school to do."

The boy was impressed. He took one more hit of the joint before passing it to his mother.

"So does this mean you're not going to tell Dad?" He asked hopefully.

"I'll mention it to him before I get my medical marijuana card. I suggest you pick one up too when you turn eighteen, your father can be a stickler for the rules, but if you find a loophole you're golden." The woman said with a strange half-cocked smile as she passed the sizzling rolled plant back to the boy.

As he French inhaled the thick, milky smoke, the boy considered mentioning the fact that his parent's allowance every week was the money he used to buy his weed. He concluded that it probably wouldn't be a good thing to bring up though at this exact moment.

"Yes ma'am. So wait, you're cool with me smoking weed?" The boy asked just to make positively sure that this wasn't a dream.

"As long as you don't get your sister involved in it and take these next few weeks of school seriously, then yeah I don't see a problem with you smoking. I expect to get in on more of your smoke sessions though. Do your friends smoke?"

The boy was feeling slightly overwhelmed. He took one more drag before passing the roach to his mother.

"Yeah well I don't know how much I want to be around you right now Mom. Don't think that just because you're smoking with me I'm all of a sudden going to forget what happened earlier. You can't bribe me like that." The boy had been thinking of a way to word his feelings towards the woman, and he figured now was as good of a time as any to let her know that she wasn't off the hook just yet.

"Yeah, I understand Jake. Listen will you at least give me the chance to explain myself?" The woman asked before killing the roach and tossing it over the fence into the neighbor's backyard.

"I guess you have a right to explain yourself. Don't give me any bullshit though I swear to God woman I can see through every lie you tell."

His mother didn't seem intimidated by the boy, instead she confidently stood up and began pacing in front of the boy.

"Alright well to start off, your father cheated on me when we first started dating, then I cheated on him once we got serious. After we were married and had you, your father felt trapped in the family dynamic, had a breakdown, and cheated on me again. In the past couple months our time in the bedroom has been rather, lacking."

"Mom. For fuck's sake." The boy interjected.

"Anyways, I met Kyle at the mall today while out shopping. He told me he'd only be in town for a couple of days though, so we grabbed lunch together in order to catch up. Kyle was always that dorky kid who I found kind of cute and innocent. And when I saw him in the mall I was so desperate I caught him like a spider does a fly."

"So you're telling me you cheated on dad because you guys aren't having sex anymore?" The boy asked, still somewhat disgusted by the fact that he was discussing his parent's sex life.

"No I slept with Kyle because I felt like your father owed me one. That coupled with the fact that he hasn't done shit in the bedroom for months broke me down. I couldn't handle it I needed attention from a man. Kyle adored me just like he used to in college. It felt good." His mother added with a sigh.

"But this? Right now? Jake this is the shittiest feeling in the world. Knowing that the one person I love the most is going to hate me for this. And who knows? He may take his ass into town the moment he finds out." His mother was beginning to despair, so the boy lit a cigarette for himself and one for his mother, which he promptly passed to her.

"Mom. You and dad low-key have one of the most fucked up marriages I've ever heard of. Why do you stay together all these years after you've both had affairs?"

"Because, Jake. Every time something like this happens and we consider splitting up, we think of you and your sister. You two little munchkins are what matter most to us, and just because we aren't a perfect couple doesn't mean we can't strive to be perfect parents."

"Well you're far from perfect let me tell you." The boy said sarcastically.

"Hey, we try." His mother replied genuinely.

"Alright mom, well I'd prefer it if you didn't bring this up with Dad until after dinner with Jfer tonight. That would be one hell of an awkward dinner."

"Good plan. Seriously though, does Jfer smoke?"

"Yes mom, she smokes weed." The boy droned as he flicked the ash off the end of his cigarette.

"Oh good, we should go for a walk after dinner and smoke together!" The woman stated enthusiastically.

"I don't know about that mom. I'll see what Jfer wants to do and I'll mention that idea to her."

"Okay hun." His mother replied softly. The boy knew his attitude only made her feel worse. He knew he should at least apologize for exploding on her, but some part of him still wanted to hold the situation over her. If he remained mad at her she would continue to try and earn his forgiveness, which in turn would provide more perks for him. Still, he couldn't help but feel sorry for the woman. She obviously already felt like shit for her actions, and him remaining outwardly sour towards her only made things worse.

He decided it was best to at least give his mother the respect she had earned as a parent. She had been the boy's caretaker for seventeen years, he owed her friendly conversation, if not outright forgiveness.

"So you haven't smoked in twenty-seven years huh?" The boy asked, trying to mask his anger with a questioning tone. He took one final drag of his cigarette and put it out in the ash tray.

"Yep, and back then the weed was maybe ten or twelve percent THC, now you kids are smoking twenty percent and higher.

It's way stronger." As she said this the woman couldn't help but giggle.

"So you're pretty high right now then, aren't you momma?" The boy said with a grin.

"You could say that." She replied happily.

If someone had told the boy earlier that day that he would be getting his mom high after school he would've never believed it. The boy found it interesting that as he grew older his life changed in major ways much more often. As he sat there talking with the woman about what it was like growing up in the seventies, he realized that he had never thought of her as a teen. The boy had always imagined the woman before him as the middle-aged mother of two that she was today. After his mother finished her cigarette she stood, gave the boy a hug, and apologized one final time for her actions. The boy could give no forgiveness but instead told her things might be okay.

The boy took a shower while the woman started to cook dinner in the kitchen. After his shower the boy got dressed and left to pick up Jfer. He had decided to pick her up earlier than they had planned in order to fill her in on all the craziness of the afternoon.

Chapter 18

The challenger pulled up to Jfer's house at five-thirty on the dot. The girl was waiting for the boy on her front porch, and sprung up as soon as he rounded the corner to her street. The moment he stopped the car she was pulling on the door handle.

"What the fuck happened? Are you okay? Why did you get pulled over?" The questions came flying as soon as she sat down.

The girl hadn't even closed the door yet and she had the boy's head spinning.

"Okay just a precursor to this conversation, I just faced a joint with my mom, I'm kind of high please don't freak me out any more than I already am." The boy replied.

"That's awesome!" The girl said excitedly. "Why'd you get pulled over though? And how'd you get out of a ticket?" She asked.

"Again with the questions. Alright so I walked in on my mom cheating on my Dad, messed the guy up, and ran. A cop stopped me on the freeway going 120 and he told me my mom had called the cops on me because I'm still technically a minor and took my parents car without permission. Turns out the officer was Mr. Jensen's brother, so he let me off easy once he understood the situation."

The girl sat in silence for a moment absorbing all the information. "So when you say you walked in on your mom?" She asked shyly.

"I walked in and heard shit but my Dad's car wasn't out front. It was some guy named Kyle that my mom knew from college."

"Ouch." The girl replied. The boy could tell that he was unloading a lot of information on her at once, and nobody wants to hear about a bunch of family crap before they make a first impression as a significant other. The boy felt bad for telling Jfer in the first place, but she had become his rock over the past couple months and he needed her right now more than ever.

"Yeah." He replied. "So we can either go back to that clusterfuck now, or we can go on that hike we've been talking about." The boy had no desire to return home as he was still shaken by the events of that afternoon, and he hoped Jfer would recognize this and opt for the hike.

"Well, why don't we just go to the park and hangout for a little while, smoke a cig and let you cool down a bit before dinner?" The girl offered.

"That sounds like a plan." The boy replied. He wasn't exactly dressed for hiking so the park was an even better idea. The girl put on her seat belt and the boy cautiously drove out of the neighborhood towards the park. If he had learned one thing from this day it was that following traffic laws was crucial.

As the car pulled into the parking lot, the boy realized just how terrible their timing was. The elementary school next door had let out a half hour ago, and the park was swarming with children running around and screaming while parents watched from a distance. Jfer suggested they walk to the bench on the far side of the park, and the boy agreed, considering he wasn't sure how much these parents would appreciate two teenagers smoking in front of their kids.

The two trudged across the grass field towards the bench in silence. While passing the playground the boy thought it was funny how these children were so excited and intoxicated by the playground. He then remembered his own excitement and intoxication on the night of his first trip. The boy concluded that perhaps all humans become jaded to their day-to-day surroundings, and all it takes is a little bit of hallucinogenic drugs to turn the boring and childish playground into a wonderland.

When they reached the bench the boy wrapped his arm around the girl and put a cigarette to his lips. Jfer turned and gave him the look that meant she wanted one as well. With a playful groan the boy handed the girl his lit cigarette and sparked a second one for himself.

"Okay, so does your dad know what happened?" The girl began after taking her first drag of the cigarette.

"Nope, not yet. Apparently my mom and he have a really fucked up relationship though. They constantly cheat on one another, it's awful. They've been doing this back and forth shit since before they were married."

"What do you mean? Like one cheats so then the other goes out and cheats?" Jfer asked with an expression of shock and what appeared to be disgust.

"Yup. They take turns having affairs. My mom felt she was owed one, so she took her hall pass to the mall and found an old friend."

"Damn hun. Well I mean at least this means they won't split up right? They've been cheating that long and they obviously still love each other despite everything that's happened." Jfer offered as an attempt to put the boy's mind at peace. It didn't help.

"Yeah, but I mean what kind of love is that?" He replied in a frustrated tone. "I mean they say they love each other and that they'll spend the rest of their lives together, but oh it's totally okay to fuck other people occasionally as long as you weren't the one to start it. They're being children about this. It's marriage! You don't cheat on someone you love that much!"

The boy was getting physically worked up, and the girl could see that talking about the subject wasn't going to calm him down any. Instead she pulled his head down onto her shoulder. Holding him down by the back of his neck she cooed and kissed the back of his head in an attempt to relax him. After about a minute the boy had calmed down enough to pick his head back up and kiss the girl.

"You're exactly what I need whenever I need it. You know that?" The boy said with a somber smile.

The girl blushed and looked away to take a drag of her cigarette. "I know." She replied with a grin before blowing her smoke straight into the boy's face.

"You're still a bitch though." The boy said with a playful grin before taking a drag of his own cancer-stick.

"Glad to see you're feeling better." The girl said before leaning in to kiss the boy's cheek.

"A little bit." The boy replied begrudgingly as he looked at his feet. He noticed a lady-bug crawling over his shoe, and while his first instinct told him to flick his foot and send the bug flying, he decided against it. Who was he to ruin the day of the little insect, after all they only had a lifetime of about two years. Every day mattered to them.

"So, random observation." The boy stated as he sat up.

"Shoot." Jfer replied as she stomped her cigarette out in the grass, barely missing the lady-bug.

"Insects and bugs are always busy you know? Like whenever you see ants they're constantly moving, they're bringing food back to the colony or whatever. I mean their entire life is based around survival. Humans aren't so different. We go to school to learn and assume our place as the most intelligent species, and then we work like ants until it's time to sit around and wait to die. In the meantime we watch as our children and our grandchildren go through the exact same process as us. It's kind of a vicious cycle don't you think?" The boy had never been one to ramble or philosophize, but seeing the ladybug made him think. They were free to fly wherever they wanted, they didn't have societal norms or expectations to live up to, and they were constantly exploring new areas.

The more the boy thought about the insect the more it dawned on him that he still felt the same way as he had as a child. He had wanted to be a bird when he grew up. Now he wanted to be a ladybug. He still felt the same constant pressure as he did before, but now he was masking his contempt towards it by playing a role he had never wanted to play. He was stuck in the loop. The same god-damned loop he had pitied not so long ago.

"Jake?" Jfer's voice snapped the boy out of his revelation.

"Shit." Was all he could muster up. The boy briefly met eyes with the girl before taking a final drag of his cigarette and flicking it into the street behind the bench. He then stood up and turned to look at the girl.

"Sorry, I just zoned out a little bit there." The boy said with a forced laugh. His entire world was crashing down around him. Who was he? What was he supposed to be in life? He damn sure didn't want to live a shitty life in a suit and tie every day. How had he found himself on this road? It was too much for the boy to handle.

"Yeah. Babe are you okay?" The girl clearly noticed something was up.

"Yeah! Sorry I just remembered that I had planned on picking up before we went back to my place for dinner, do you have your card?" The boy thanked his creators for his quick wit and ability to bullshit.

Jfer seemed suspicious at first, but the boy figured she wouldn't think too hard about it considering how much they smoked. "Alright, well yeah I have my card, where do you want to go? One-Xix?" The girl asked as she stood and walked towards the boy. When she stopped in front of him the boy pulled her in for a kiss and took her hands in his. They stood like this for a moment, just two stupid kids stuck in love. Then the boy intertwined his fingers with the girls and led the way towards the car.

"Yeah One-Six will work." He said with a smile in the girl's direction. The sight of her smiling back hit him like a Mack truck. No longer was she his perfect girlfriend, she was an elaborate ruse set out before him. Jfer was safe, comfortable, and normal. Everything the boy had found wrong in the world. How could he have allowed himself to break like this? He had changed too much, he had broken and followed the crowd. Now that he saw a glimpse of what he would be leaving it called to him, begging him not to go.

The drive to the clinic was drowned out by Jfer scanning the radio for a station with decent music. The boy was in limbo. He didn't know what he wanted in life or where he was going. However, he knew that he wanted a couple grams of purp and that he was currently driving towards the clinic. All he could do was put one foot in front of the other and watch what happened as he tumbled down the stairs he had sprinted up.

As they pulled into the parking lot the boy pulled out thirty dollars and handed the bills to Jfer. The girl took the money and grabbed her purse before opening the car door.

"Be right back" She said with a smile.

"Hmm-kay" the boy replied as he looked down at his phone. As the passenger door closed with a thud, the boy had an adrenaline fueled instinct to leave. To leave Jfer at the clinic, peal out of the parking lot, and drive until he hit open road. However, something calmed him. The boy wasn't sure if it was the comforting thoughts and memories of the time he had already spent with Jfer, or if it was the fact that they were both at a point in their lives where falling out of love wasn't ideal. Graduation was just around the corner, and along with it plenty of summer activities involving both Jfer and the group of kids the boy had become friends with.

The boy wanted to know why now—of all times—he was reminded of his true nature and mindset. Maybe with the threat of college coming his subconscious panicked and tried to push the boy back towards his original factory settings. Maybe he was at the point where he had to choose between one life and the other. Either way, the boy knew he couldn't handle this situation immaturely. Ditching Jfer at the clinic and running off in search of freedom wouldn't be the most responsible thing to do, and regardless of how his renewed sense of entrapment tugged at him to flee, the boy knew he had responsibilities to handle first.

Jfer returned before long carrying a white bag for prescriptions, and as she slinked into the passenger seat she dropped the open bag onto the boys lap.

"Three grams of purp, like you asked. They tossed in a free peanut butter cup, it's supposedly pretty potent." The girl said with a grin before pulling her seatbelt on.

"Thank you babe." The boy crooned as he picked through the contents of the bag. "Was Nate working today?" The boy asked as he plucked the peanut butter cup edible out of the bag. Their mutual friend Nate had been working at this particular clinic for the past month, and would often hook up his friends with deals.

"No dude it was this bombass chick with a sleeve tattoo." The girl replied before adding "She must have been new, because I haven't seen her before."

"Oh, well apparently you have a crush on her. Should I be worried?" The boy replied with a snicker before unwrapping the peanut butter cup and offering half to the girl.

"For the pre-dinner nerves." He said with a smile.

"Jake this will kick in like right as we're sitting down for dinner." The girl scoffed.

The boy popped his half of the edible in his mouth and shifted the car into drive. "Even better, it's for the mid-meal munchies. Make sure to compliment my mother's cooking afterwards."

The girl's laughter was soon replaced by music. Neither of them had much to say it seemed, and any attempt at talking ended in an awkward silence. They both had too much on their mind to be distracted by conversation. The boy preferred things this way, and it was part of the reason he liked Jfer so much. The girl was obviously nervous as all hell for dinner, and the new information the boy had dropped on her probably wasn't helping her feel any more confident about the situation.

On the other hand, the boy was caught up in his own thoughts. What was he supposed to do next? Make it through dinner? What happened after dinner when his mother broke the news to his father? While the boy knew he couldn't possibly have all the answers at that exact moment, it frustrated him that he didn't have even the slightest form of control over the situation.

The boy believed this was what he deserved for feeling close to the people around him. He had made a connection with his cousin Michael, and had ended up hurt. He had instinctively made a connection with his parents and now he was being hurt for it. He had made a connection with Jfer and now he already had one foot out the door emotionally. He didn't want to be hurt by her. He was tired of being hurt by every single person he made a connection with.

His restless train of thought was broken by the approaching driveway. The boy slowly pulled the challenger up the cracked slab of concrete and parked the car in his usual spot. His father's car was in its normal spot, which the boy took as a sign that his mother had kept her word and reserved comment on the affair for after dinner. Knowing his father, the first reaction would be to walk out and drive straight down to the local bar to drink away the news.

"Alright, are you ready to enter the wolf den?" The boy said with a half-cocked smile aimed in the girl's direction.

"Well shit what's the worst that happens? I screw up dinner and then your parents forget about it due to the fact that they have bigger problems to deal with? I really don't have much to lose here with a bad impression." As the girl said this she gave the boy a falsely-confident grin and stepped out of the car.

"That's the spirit!" The boy called as she closed the door behind him. Jfer certainly knew how to act the part of a good girlfriend, and as the boy stepped out of the car he couldn't help but notice that she looked the part as well.

"You look, phenomenal." The boy said quietly as the girl stopped under the orange glow of the street-light. Remnants of the evening sun still hung in the sky, giving the front yard a dusk-like blue aura. There Jfer stood, outlined by the blue of the night air and glowing with the orange of the street light. The boy was transfixed. How could he have not said something earlier?

The girl let out a short laugh and did a quick twirl, allowing the bottom of her dress to erupt out in a circle around her. The pink dress seemed to shimmer, which only brought more attention to the gleam in her eyes. They had always been the most beautiful aspect of the girl in his opinion, they seemed to pierce into him, almost as if they could peek into his soul.

Impossible, the boy thought. There was no way that the girl would be giving him that look of affection if she knew what he was weighing on his soul right now.

"I mean it babe. Sometimes I think I'm the luckiest guy in the world." The boy couldn't hold himself back anymore, it didn't matter if she was some ruse to keep him stuck in a vicious cycle. This girl in front of him represented beauty. Not in the sense that Jfer was hot. She was gorgeous to say the least, but it was more than that. She had a presence of life, an aura that gave away her attitude; "we are here for only so long. Might as well make the most of it."

"Jake, you've got to stop looking at me like that." The girl said, breaking the spell her smile had on him.

"Like what?" The boy said, but before Jfer could answer, the front door opened and the boy's mother came shuffling out with a wide grin.

"Hi Jennifer! How are you sweetheart?" The woman asked with sincerity. Her tone sickened the boy.

Chapter 19

Dinner went surprisingly smooth. Any awkward pauses in conversation were filled with the sounds of silverware tinking against the plates. Jfer did an excellent job handling the boy's parents. Even though it was difficult for her and the boy to look Mr. Rivera in the eyes, somehow the topic of the affair was never revealed. Maura—the boy's little sister—was obsessed with Jfer. Jake could almost see the awe in the younger girl's eyes.

To be fair this was the first girl the boy had ever brought home to introduce to his family, and Jfer was doing splendidly. His sister would later tell him that she thought he was gay for all those years, and that she was even suspicious that Jfer was a cover-up because she did so well with her first impression.

Regardless of how well the dinner went, the boy couldn't help but notice the gnawing feeling in his stomach begging him to run. The entire meal felt like a form of purgatory. The boy knew the conversation between his mom and dad could either end badly, meaning they continue their screwed-up relationship, or terribly, meaning they get a divorce. Either way the coin flipped, his allusion of love had forever been shattered. The two people who had exemplified true love in his life were in fact, liars.

It was a sobering thought for the boy. He wondered how Jfer felt about love, considering her parents were already divorced. What if the girl didn't believe in love anymore? What if there wasn't such a thing as a "true love."

The boy thought about all of this while keeping up light conversation with the other people around the dinner table. Maybe his definition of love was flawed? Could it be that love is not about being perfect with someone, but instead about loving their imperfections just as much as they love yours? The boy's head was starting to hurt, he needed to stop thinking so hard on the subject or it would only get him more and more worked up.

After dinner the boy and his father took care of cleaning the dishes while the girls sat outside by the fire pit.

"Jfer seems like a pretty nice girl Jake. I'm glad you brought her over for us to finally meet." The boy's father began as his sponge slicked across the plate.

"Thanks dad, I'm happy you and mom approve." The boy replied before taking the plate from his father and placing it in the dishwasher.

"Yeah, I mean it seems like she's a very mature young lady. And by that I mean she appears to know what she wants from life. Maybe she's wise beyond her years or just blessed to know what she wants, but I think that's one of the greatest attributes someone your age can have." His father continued, swishing the sponge and rinsing the suds.

"Do you think I have that attribute?" The boy asked challengingly.

"No son, you don't." The man answered before handing the boy a rinsed plate for the dishwasher.

"Why not?" Inquired the boy as he took the plate and set it in the dishwasher forcefully.

"I don't know. Your kid-sister has it, the girl's a straight-A student who knows what she wants to do and is taking the steps towards making that happen. Some people are given a staircase in life son, others—like you and me—are thrown into this world blind as shit with a decent set of skills and some rope." The man said gruffly as he handed the boy the final dish.

The boy pondered his father's philosophy for a second while he set the last plate in the dishwasher. After thinking about it for a second, the boy replied. "So what's the rope for?" His father was getting preachy and the boy always had trouble following when the man spoke in esoteric metaphors.

This was greeted with a chuckle as his father began to dry his hands. "Well, you tie that rope to other people, and eventually you have enough people tied together so that as a cumulative effort, all of you reach the end safely. I'll tell you this now son- you try and stumble through this life alone, and you'll find yourself stuck in all kinds of shit. You tie yourself to a few people like Jfer or your sister, and they'll take you straight to the Promised Land."

The boy was at a loss for words. He had always known his father was a wise man, but this was still a startling revelation for the boy. It made sense, that if you wanted to reach an end-goal you should tag along with other people. But then again, what if he didn't want the same life as them. What if he didn't want the normal "American Dream" middle-class family? What if he wanted more from his life? Was he doomed to wander blindly until he stumbled upon something glorious? Or more likely wander blindly until his conformity or death?

The funniest part about the whole conversation was that Jfer was anything but your average goal-oriented girl. Sure she had goals, and was determined to achieve them. But at the same time the girl was a total free-spirit. As the boy gazed out on her through the kitchen window he smiled. Jfer was the type who was going to go far in the world. The boy understood now. Her free-spirit and independence combined with her beauty and passion would put her in the upper-echelon of society.

It saddened the boy to realize Jfer had been wasting her potential with him and the rest of squad. She was the kind of girl who lit up a room when she walked in, why was she hiding herself among the druggies and hoes of high school? She was like a tigress hunting alongside hyenas.

"So who did you tie yourself to?" The boy asked as his father began to walk away, causing the man to turn around with a strange look on his face.

"Your mother." He replied with a smile. "After we got married her father was the one who helped my business expand as much as it did. It's good to have a suga-momma." The man said as he shuffled his feet in an attempt to dance.

"Oh God, dad stop. Well thanks for the life lesson. I think Jfer likes you guys too."

"Yeah no problem kiddo, now let's rejoin the ladies, shall we?" The man replied as he opened the sliding glass door leading to the backyard.

"Yeah, give me a sec though I forgot my pack in the car." The boy said as he turned in the direction of the front door. "I'll meet you out there."

"Alright sounds good." His father called after him.

The boy had to get out of the presence of his father. This man owed a lot to his mother and her family, they had done much for his business. He remembered as a kid when his grandfather would come home from work with his father occasionally. He had always assumed his grandfather worked with his dad, but maybe his grandfather had been helping his old man run the business. All of this was insignificant compared to the thought of his mother cheating on this man who worked his ass off to keep her happy.

Regardless of how the conversation turned out between his mother and father, the boy knew one thing. He could never look at marriage the same way again. His father married his mother in the hopes of providing a good life for her. He had swallowed his pride and let her father come in and help him, and she cheated on him as repayment. But then again his father had cheated on his mother before. It was awful, the boy couldn't stand the thought of it. Here he was finally thinking he had found love in the world, and his parents were crushing the model he based love off of.

He stumbled his way down to the driveway in a stupor. He had no desire to return inside, as there was nothing for him in the house besides broken dreams. "No." The boy thought. "I'm being dramatic, this isn't a big deal, just a part of growing up, right? First Santa, then the tooth fairy, and now love. Fuck. I can't wait to be an adult."

The boy angrily slammed his fist onto the top of the challenger, and immediately regretted it after pulling his hand back in pain. For what it was worth, the car had a decently-sized divot just above the driver's side window. The boy felt bad, but then again he doubted his parents would worry too much about a divot in the car when he explained to them how he got himself out of a speeding ticket.

After unlocking the car and grabbing his cigarettes out of the center console, the boy closed the door and sparked up on the driveway. He needed a minute to calm down and collect his thoughts. As he leaned against the car and took a drag of his cigarette the boy was reminded of a famous quote from Tumblr, "Inhale the good shit, exhale the bullshit."

In the boy's case, the good shit was a cancerous combination of bleached paper, tobacco, nicotine, and other tasty chemicals. The bad shit was his anger towards his parents, the anxiety about what this day meant for the future of his family, and the fear of what a world without love could mean.

The boy's instincts told him to jump into the car and drive. To drive until he ran out of gas money and start over wherever he ended up. He could feel his fingers twitching with anticipation. The moment was coming, all he had to do was pull the handle and jump into the driver's seat. His body would go on autopilot from there and take him to wherever he was heading.

"Hey." The voice came from the side yard. The boy craned his neck and squinted his eyes to see around the dark corner of the house. Jfer was standing coolly in the darkness with one leg propped up against the wall. The boy wasn't sure how long the girl had been standing there, but judging by the look she gave him as she stepped out of the darkness he figured she had witnessed his outburst of anger.

"So they're kinda waiting for you back there." Jfer said in a cautious tone as she approached the boy.

"I had to grab my pack." The boy replied sheepishly.

"Babe are you okay?" The girl asked as she looked up at the boy with her luminescent eyes.

"Yeah! No I'm fine, don't even trip." It was a shitty lie and the boy knew it. The girl shot him a look as if she didn't believe him, but the boy cut the look off by leaning in and kissing her.

"Here." The boy said as he handed the cigarette to the girl.

"That's not really what I want right now." The girl replied as she wrapped her arms around his torso.

There was just something about the girl, even the way her head rested against his chest made the boy feel at ease. He wasn't particularly muscular, but her body squeezing against his in the warm air of an early summer night made him feel like the biggest person in the world. What he felt towards the girl might not have been love, but he knew deep down it was something. The boy didn't know it yet, but this exact moment in time was when young Jennifer began to slowly tie her noose around the boy's heart.

"Alright you caught me." The boy mumbled between the strands of hair that he had rested his lips on.

"Mhm. You can't hide your feelings from me dumbass. I see right through you." As Jfer said this she looked up and cracked a sincere smile.

The boy paused for a moment to avert his gaze from the girl and instead began to stare out aimlessly into the night sky. After a final deep breath to calm himself and collect his thoughts, he began to speak.

"I don't know. I've always had this grand idea of what love is, and what it looks like. After all the shit that went down today, I'm not even sure if love is a real thing. And honestly, even if it is real, how the fuck can we ever expect to find it when we're surrounded by so many false ideas of it. I mean Jesus, Jfer. Look at the news, all you see is crap about how some celebrity loves another one and then three months later the two are in an all-out custody war. That's not love." Jfer cut the boy off here by asking a question he hadn't been expecting.

"Jake what do you think love is? I don't mean what you see from love on the TV, or in books, or in music. But when you think of love, what do you think of?"

The boy took a minute to consider the question. He hadn't really thought about it much, and now that the girl was bringing it to his attention he had never really put a firm definition on love.

"Well, I used to think love was coming home every day to a happy home and a beautiful woman who loves and adores you. As simple as that."

"So Adam will never find love in your opinion?" The girl asked with a snicker.

"I don't think Adam will ever find anyone who loves him more than himself to be quite honest with you." The boy retorted before continuing on. "What I'm trying to say is that I thought love was being completely comfortable with someone. You know? You can come home every day and they'll be there to celebrate your wins and help you push past your losses. Someone who will be your biggest fan when you want it, and your only fan when you need it. I guess I thought love was about being there for someone and caring for them, but knowing that they're putting forth the same effort and feelings towards you."

There was a pause after the boy had finished, and he wondered if his views had offended Jfer in some way.

"It's funny." The girl replied, "You come from a two-parent home, so that's what you're used to. Your idea of love is based off of your parents. If I had based my idea of love off of my parents I would think that love is about sending a monthly check and cussing out your children in the hopes they wouldn't become like you."

The boy realized he had struck a chord with Jfer. It was true, he had been blessed to have a privileged upbringing in a two-parent household. Jfer's father had been the lead guitarist in an almost-famous 80's rock band. After the time of rock and roll died out, he cut his hair and got a business degree which he had used to start up his own music shop. After a few years the business took off, and so did he.

"The thing is though," Jfer continued, "I didn't get my perspective of love from anybody in particular, as a matter of fact, I'm not even sure I know what love looks like. But that's not a bad thing." The boy gave the girl a questioning look.

"I mean come on, we're eighteen. Or at least I am. You're still jailbait for a couple weeks. But love doesn't show itself when you're eighteen, and it doesn't show itself when you're ninety either. I don't even believe love *can* be seen, it's felt. Like think about that first night of camping. Yes, we were all royally trashed, but the vibes were good, the people were happy, and the love was felt. Love is that warm feeling you get when you're surrounded by people you care about. It has nothing to do with what you do for them, or what they do for you. It's about the mutual connection you share with people, it's about coming together over a common thing. So if you think your parents don't love each other, I think you're wrong. Just because your mom cheated on your Dad doesn't mean they're heading to splittsville. Maybe your mom's just an attention whore?"

"Alright take it easy on my mom." The boy interjected half-heartedly. Jfer had a point, and regardless of whether it was for attention or for sex, his mother had been "whorish" to say the least that day.

"I love your mom, Jake. I love your whole family. But what I'm trying to point out to you is that adults aren't infallible. They make the same mistakes we do sometimes, they're still learning just like us. They still make mistakes just like us. Love isn't about the perfections. It's about taking all of the imperfections you see in someone and saying 'I don't care.' Love's about learning to lose it all, and then realizing that what you have left is what really matters."

"Pretty well thought-out theory for an eighteen year old, don't you think?" The boy asked sarcastically. The girl made a good point, but he wasn't sure he wanted to accept a whole new version of love just yet. He needed time for the haze to lift.

"Well I like to think I'm a pretty enlightened person, you should hear my opinion on same-sex marriage, Adam thinks I should go into politics for gay rights."

"Oh lord. Well let's just keep that argument to yourself for the night. My parents are pretty hard-nosed conservative when it comes to that kind of stuff."

"Fair enough, so Bush jokes wouldn't be appropriate either?" Jfer asked with a mischievous grin.

"Thank God you're good at hiding this side from my parents." The boy replied as he leaned in for another kiss.

"Speaking of parents I'm supposed to be talking to them right now, not you. Come on let's head back."

"Alright, well just one last thing before we go." The boy said sheepishly.

"And what would that one last thing be?" Jfer asked as she slowly tugged the boy's jacket towards her in the direction of the sideyard.

"I may not have a definition of love to give you anymore, but whatever it may be- I think I feel it. And I think I like it." As the boy said this he reached forward, grabbed the girl by the waist, and pulled her into a deep kiss.

For a moment the two teenagers stood there frozen in their space of time. Their moment of unending bliss. As he kissed the girl the boy felt everything. Every crack in her dried lips, the belt loop around her waist that was hanging on by a single thread, the constant, steady beat of her heart. It was almost melodic the way they stood on the driveway. Hoping against hope that the spark they found in each other would be enough to illuminate the darkness around them.

At one point the boy remembered that the rest of his family was waiting in the backyard for them. With reluctance he detached himself from the longing lips of Jfer and rested his forehead against hers. The girl took in a shallow, shaky breath before speaking.

"Nobody's ever kissed me like that before." Was all the girl could squeak out before she wrapped her arms even tighter around the boy.

"Nobody's ever made me feel like you do." Was all the boy had to say for himself.

The two shared another brief moment of silence before agreeing to rejoin the others in the backyard. The boy wrapped one hand around the girl's waist and flicked his forgotten cigarette into the street with the other. After one final kiss he led the way down the side-yard towards the time bomb that had been left sitting in the backyard.

Chapter 20

The boy awoke to the smell of burning cannabis and a vision of beer bottles and bodies scattered across a grey fuzzy carpet. He sensed a presence behind him and upon reaching back felt the familiar leather bracelet that was wrapped around the wrist of the girl he loved. Jfer had fallen asleep big spooning the boy. It was beginning to come back to him.

The grey fuzzy carpet he was lying on belonged to Adam, and the bodies and bottles could be explained by the uncontrollable and barbaric graduation party that had occurred the previous night. The boy knew he had been drinking for much of the day post-ceremony, but his memory of the party that continued into the night was splotchy at best.

Slowly pulling himself partially from the haze of the night before and partially from the soft, warm embrace of his girlfriend, the boy scanned the room for signs of life. Adam was perched in the windowsill of the den, a spot he had deemed his throne. The morning—strike that—early afternoon light was streaming in through the glass window pane. It painted a cool blue and white pattern across Adam's sunburnt face and shirtless torso. The boy reached for his phone and took a photo, as Adam would probably get a hard-on for the potential new twitter profile picture.

As he gently tapped the small grey camera button his phone let off an obnoxiously loud clicking noise, causing the subject of the photo to stir from his slumber and turn towards the boy. He cautiously cracked open his eyes to the sunlight beaming in through his throne's window.

"Is that really necessary?" Adam mumbled as he rested a forearm over his eyes to block out the blinding beams of light.

"I'm sorry, I forgot you're the selfie queen. It's a pretty dope picture though." The boy responded as he pulled himself into a sitting position.

"Send it to me." Adam replied back lazily. The boy quickly opened up his messages and sent Adam the picture he had taken. Knowing it would take a moment to reach his friend across the room, he decided to probe Adam's mind for any possible answers to what had occurred the night before.

"Soooo. Did you black out last night too?"

"Yeah." Adam paused for a moment. "Pretty sure I swooped up on a bag of Xanies that some kid left in the garage. And then took several of them." With this Adam squeezed his eyes tightly shut and shook his head violently in an attempt to clear the dark clouds left over from a night of being barred out.

"No, you started the night with the bag of Xanies, remember? Then you ended up trading them with Nate for the magnum bottle of champagne he brought."

Adam took a moment to process the possible error in his memory, but upon looking down at the windowsill between his outstretched legs, his face lit up in delight.

"Lookie here son!" Adam said with a boyish grin. "I am the come-up God." His grin warped into a proud smirk as he held up a snack-sized plastic baggie with three small white pills inside.

The boy stared in awe of Adam for a moment. The kid could go into a party without a drop of beer to his name and leave with two bottles and drugs to boot. It was a scary trait, but impressive nonetheless.

"Story." The boy stated excitedly. It was a form of ritual for the group. Every night they recorded the craziest and most legendary moments on their Snapchat story. The next morning when their memories were wiped *Men in Black* style, each member of the group would start by watching their own story. Once they had a general idea of what they did the night before, they proceeded to watch the stories of other members of the group that had been at the same party. This was a tried-and-true method of getting every piece of a night back together so nobody would end up with *Hangover* nights.

The first picture, a selfie with Jfer and Coronas poolside the previous afternoon. The second, a video of Adam jumping in the pool with his cap and gown on. The third, a video of four cars full of squad members and close friends pulling into Adams wrap-around driveway. A picture of Adam presenting the truckload of alcohol he had bought for the party. The stash included two kegs, three bottles of Ciroq, two bottles of Jose, several different types of chasers and mixers, and two "well-aged" (according to Adam) bottles of wine.

The next couple videos brought a smile to the boy's face. Jfer had clearly stolen his phone at some point and was running around the party handing out shots to the party guests. Soon the stories took a wilder turn as the night progressed and more people began pouring into the house. At one point the boy took a video from the balcony overlooking the backyard. At least one-hundred people were scattered throughout the pool and fire pits, and more were pouring out of the house. The next story took a terrifying turn involving a bottle being thrown in the direction of Adam's father.

Then cop lights, beer pong, dancing, another selfie with Jfer, people leaving en-mass, the squad smoking, the champagne bottle coming out, Nate passed out (most likely the Xanax). The boy had seen enough to paint a pretty vivid picture of the night in his head.

"Damn." The boy said as he looked up to see Adam smiling at his phone.

"Yeah, that was a good one." Adam replied contentedly. That was one thing the boy had always admired about Adam, no matter how big the party was, no matter how crazy the night was, Adam always kept a cool demeanor in regards to his partying antics. A modern-day Gatsby without a Daisy (or Tom in this case).

The two slowly pieced the night together after going through their friends' Snapchat stories. Occasionally one of them would make a comment on a video or picture, and the other would either laugh or comment on that particular memory that had until recently been lost in the void of the night before.

As more members of the squad began to awake from their drunken sleep, stories were swapped. The boy decided to roll a joint with the weed left over on the coffee table. There was nothing better for a hangover than a wake and bake. Nate had stretched out across the couch and was drooling on his shoulder, so the boy shook him awake and convinced him to sit up.

Despite being the first person to pass out according to the stories, Nate seemed to remember the most out of everyone in the group. However he seemed to forget the fact that Adam had stolen his drugs, so Adam tossed the little baggie back to him.

Jfer finally arose from her sleep as the boy was sealing up the joint he had scraped together.

"Good morning." The boy said with a smile as Jfer cautiously pulled herself onto the couch next to him.

"Good timing." The girl replied with a kiss.

"Mm. Morning breath." The boy said with a smirk, eliciting a sigh of annoyance from his girlfriend.

The boy sparked the joint and passed it first to Jfer. "This should help with that, and the pounding headache you probably have going right now."

"Ugh. Yes please, and thank you." Jfer said as she plucked the joint from the boy's fingertips.

A burst of movement on his left caused the boy to see Nate sprinting towards the bathroom as Adam laughed hysterically.

"You good Nate?" The boy called after him with a chuckle. Nates only response was to slam the bathroom door shut behind him.

"He might want to hurry up." Jfer said after taking a hit of the J. "I can feel the fireball fighting my empty stomach right now and it is not comfortable."

The boy dramatically leapt off the seat to a safe distance away from Jfer's puke-radius.

"Hey! I'm not about to puke on you for Christ's sake. I just need some breakfast and I'll be fine. Adam do you want to hit this?"

Adam rose from his throne and collected the joint from Jfer on the other side of the room.

"Thank you, and I'm starved to be honest, we should grab some breakfast burritos. Jake you down to drive?"

"Yeah I think I have gas, let's wait until Nate gets out of the bathroom though, some greasy food would probably help whatever's going on in there." As the boy said this all three nervously looked in the direction of the bathroom.

The joint was passed around a few times, and many of the random party guests who had passed out found their way to the front door before Nate finally re-emerged from the bathroom. He walked slowly, precariously tiptoeing his way towards the couch so as not to further upset his queasy stomach.

"You good homie?" The boy asked as Nate plopped down without a sliver of the grace and tenderness he had had before.

"Not too shabby. Feeling better now, thanks." Nate replied with a calm deep breath.

"Breakfast burrito?" Inquired the boy as he handed what was left of the joint to his companion.

Nate took a hit and blew the smoke out, leaning his head back slowly until it came to rest against the wall behind the couch. After closing his eyes for a moment that caused the rest of the group to exchange looks of concern, Nate responded. "Down. Greasiness is key right now." With this, the group found themselves slowly making their way through the house and out into the fresh salty air. The view that greeted the boy was like something out of a *Sublime* music video.

The party had been thrown at the beach house owned by Adam's family, and it was magnificent. The house was located in a private cove just north of Marina del Rey, there were only three neighbors in the entire cove, and each of them was a seasonal renter. So the only other person for miles was an elderly Chinese man who could often be seen standing on his porch overlooking the ocean, or meditatively pacing the shoreline.

Jfer took the boy's hand as they trudged through the sand towards a large stone staircase leading to the residential parking lot. The beach they were walking along was in a sense privately owned by Adam's family. Looking out across it made the boy contemplate just how much money the family really had- and how they had really earned it. The boy didn't know much about what Mr. and Mrs. King did, but the expansiveness of their resources, connections, and getaways like this drew a little bit too much attention for the boy to not notice.

Lately it had become a running joke for the group to comment on how Adam's parents were such professional drug dealers while Adam was simply terrible. Regardless of how they earned the money, the boy was just happy they did. He was blessed to have met Adam, the places he had been and the things he had been able to do were incredible. While the boy stepped assertively across the sandy beach with his fingers intertwined with Jfer's, he was reminded of the hike they had gone on a few months ago during their camping trip.

At one point Jfer and the boy had gotten themselves wildly lost and hadn't been sure where they were or how far they were from the campsite. It had been a miracle they made it back that day, pure luck more than anything else. All the better, he made a figure of himself by guiding the way back to camp, even though Jfer was the one who was supposed to be familiar with the area. He had guided her with a single hand then just as he was now. Confident in his sense of direction. Jfer didn't agree with the sexist idea of a man's "natural" sense of direction. She made this point quite clear on several occasions when the boy had been guiding her back to the campsite on that early spring evening.

Nevertheless, Jfer also knew how much the boy enjoyed feeling dominant in the face of a relationship where each person's opinions and thoughts were weighed equally. In times like these where the boy insisted on playing the male stereotype, she let him have it. He played his part well and it was fun for her to slip into "basic girlfriend" mode from time to time.

As the staircase approached the boy acknowledged it's presence with a simple curse word. The staircase led nearly vertically up a cliff at least five stories. It was a beautiful walk down into the cool breeze of the cove, but a bitch of a hike if you were on your way back up.

The group began the ascent with groans of protest that died down by about the third flight of stairs. The lungs of a smoker aren't made for rapid elevation change, and the group was quickly out of breath.

"Adam, I love your house man. You white-peopled the shit out of that thing man, all the fancy home décor." *Gasp for breath* "But can't you just get a long hill leading down as a driveway or something?" *Pant* "Fuck these stairs bruh I'm dying!"

And with that the group stopped two flights of stairs short of the parking lot. All of them gripping their sides from the combination of laughter and their own shortness of breath. It was a potent combination, which required approximately two minutes of recovery where bellies and sides were stretched, balls were itched, and loogies were spat.

After pulling themselves together once more for the final leg, the group rose onto the parking lot as a victorious Olympic sprinter does when going for the gold. Left breathless from the last-minute dash to the top for first place, and the celebration that followed afterwards, the four teens walked to the car gasping for breath between sideways glances at each other and laughter.

The boy drove for the group and Jfer filled the passenger seat. It felt good for him to be able to hold the girl's hand as he drove. Almost like he was an adult. Then again, he was an adult now. The boy's birthday had been earlier that week! While the celebration on that evening had been spectacular, it paled in comparison to the day he had spent with Jfer. A day off of school due to senior finals the week before had given them the perfect opportunity to catch the sunrise on the boy's balcony and enjoy a day by the pool while his father was at work. Even better- his mother had claimed she "owed him one" and took a spa day for herself, on the condition that the boy didn't enter their room or touch their bed.

His mother had given them two rules, so naturally both had been broken during the first thirty seconds following the woman's departure. The sex had been incredible, the weed Jfer had brought him as a birthday present made him feel free as a bird, and summer was within reach. It had been a perfect day.

This day was not a perfect day. The boy didn't have enough gas to reach the burrito stand the group had been so keen on visiting, so Taco Bell was forced to suffice. Along the way Jfer had seemed off-put and a touch irritable. She got in moods like this often where she wouldn't say more than a few words for hours at a time, and originally the boy had thought it was a sign of affection, like she was at peace somehow. Now he saw the standoffishness for what it really was- annoyance.

The boy thought it was irritating how in the grand scheme of things little chips in the girl's armor shouldn't matter much, but in the day-to-day scheme of things, things like this were slowly becoming a rift in the relationship. The boy felt it, he had simply chosen not to acknowledge the distance growing between him and his girlfriend.

After the second-choice food had been stomached and post-meal cigarettes had been enjoyed by all, the group returned to Adam's beach house to plan out their day. Two other members of the squad arrived shortly after the group returned. And a smoke session was held in honor of the festivities from the night before. When it was time to get down to business, Adam casually called the group to attention.

"Alright, so what are we doing today?" He asked with a questioning tone. Adam used simple eye contact to convince others in the room to offer input. It was a handy trait of his, one instinct that helped make him a natural-born leader.

"How's about a day off?" Nate offered hopefully from the couch.

"Nooooo days off pussy!" Adam responded.

"Well what if we just hungout around here and relaxed?" Jfer said, acknowledging the need for a rest day.

"I say we hit Santa Monica and Venice." The boy jumped in. The look he received from Jfer told him this wasn't the right choice, but he also knew he didn't want to be around her in this mood.

"There you go Jake! Now we're coming up with some real ideas!" Adam encouraged.

The boy had an idea for a surprise he might be able to bring home from Santa Monica, but wasn't sure if it was realistic or if his expectations would be shattered due to wallet constraints.

"Well I for one can't handle another day out in the sun." Piped in Alex, one of the girls that had arrived that morning at the beach house. She had been a constant at the house over the past couple days.

At this point Adam turned to the boy. "Well Jake, you want to hit Santa Monica and Venice and be back by sunset to throw some burgers on the grill?"

"What, you don't think I can throw some burgers on the grill?" Nate interjected, clearly offended.

"No. Nate I know for a fact that you can't, and even if you could, you would eat them all because you're a fucking fatass." Adam replied with a sassy smile. Nate wasn't much bigger than

Adam, but he was much more muscular, which Adam refused to acknowledge.

Nate replied by chucking a half-eaten SlimJim across the room which connected with the side of Adam's head.

"Alright so Santa Monica, let's go Jake." Adam said, shaking off the blow to his head.

"You want to just leave now?" The boy said with a look in Jfer's direction.

"Well yeah we have to stop along the way to get gas, right?" Adam said with continued enthusiasm.

"Yeah, but it's one-thirty and I'm high and need to take a shower. Let's go at two." The boy countered.

"Alright, let me know when you're ready to go then." Adam said in response. The boy pulled Jfer up off the seat next to him and took off in the direction of his temporary bedroom. The two could hear cries of "finally, get a room" and Nate fake-vomiting between chuckles.

"Finally got you on my own." Jfer said soothingly as the boy pulled her into the bedroom and shut the door behind them.

"Well enjoy it you won't have me for long." The boy replied as he pulled the girl in for a kiss. The girl kissed back at first, but retreated after moment with a puzzled look on her face.

"So why do you have to go to Santa Monica with Adam? Can't we just spend another day together like your birthday?" As she said this Jfer seductively traced her fingertips down the boy's back.

"I need to check something out, I should come home with a nice surprise though if all works out." The boy answered with a smile. He knew it hurt Jfer to watch him deny her for reasons unknown to her, and it felt wrong for him to not keep her in the loop about such a major life choice. But for whatever reason, the boy had decided to keep his tattoo under wraps.

He had talked to Natalie—Mr. Jensen's girlfriend—after graduation and she had given him the name and address of the tattoo shop she worked at in Santa Monica. The boy had called in the previous day to schedule an appointment with Natalie. Perhaps she was the reason the boy had been okay with leaving Jfer behind. The boy knew he was attracted to her, she was beautiful in a different way, and it intrigued him. Regardless of how he thought of the woman she was six years his elder and way out of his league. The boy decided not to think too hard about the beautiful tatted-up goddess that awaited him while he undressed first himself then his girlfriend.

The couple stumbled their way into the shower and began to rinse off. During a pause filled with passionate kissing the lights went out in the bathroom. While they both had a general sense of where the shampoo bottles were, the teens stood for a moment in quiet panic. Clutching each other tightly in the dark as water streamed down their bodies, they began to laugh. Obviously their friends were having a laugh in the bedroom. One downside of the bathrooms in Adam's house was that they light switches were located outside the door, and there were no windows to let natural light into the room.

The lights remained off for a couple minutes, so the boy took full advantage of the beautiful girlfriend that had decided to accompany him into the shower. By the time the lights turned on both individuals were lying in a heap on the floor laughing. Throwing subtlety out the window the boy had accidentally knocked one of the bottles of soap off the small nook in the wall where it had been resting. The bottle had taken a tumble straight down onto Jfer's toe, prompting the girl to reel in pain and slip, falling to the floor and taking the boy's legs out from under him in the process.

As the couple re-gathered their wits in the phosphorescent artificial light they both noticed the shower door gaping open, allowing water to splash out and onto the floor which collected in small pools and trickled towards the door. The boy rose first and closed the door before pulling his girlfriend to her feet and sniping a kiss and an ass grab. He had learned there were really only two things the girl constantly needed, attention through kisses and assertiveness through a firm hand on the booty.

After finishing their shower the two stepped out and dried off. The boy poked his head out first to see if any of the other houseguests were waiting outside with a paintball gun or some other terrible addition to their prank. After confirming that there were no immediate threats in the bedroom he cautiously darted over to the door and twisted the lock into place.

"That would have been a better idea about ten minutes ago when we first got in here." Jfer said smoothly from behind the boy. As he turned around his eyes grew wide with astonishment. His girlfriend stood awkwardly in the doorway between the bathroom and the bedroom. The girl worked hard for her body and she was proud of it, innocently posing naked against the doorframe, biting her nail. The pin-up model pose she was striking only helped to accentuate her curvature.

The boy couldn't help but be distracted by the girl, so when he emerged from the bedroom a quarter past two he greeted Adam with a smirk and a sarcastic apology. The drive took only thirty minutes with a ten minute pit stop for cigarettes and gas. Adam's first stop was Venice beach, as the supply of weed was running thin and Venice provided an assortment of clinics and dispensaries.

After venturing into a few clinics the boy decided to spend a little money early and invest in his medicinal marijuana recommendation. After a few questions and seventy-five dollars the boy had a piece of paper that would allow him to buy medicinal-grade weed from any clinic in California. The process took forty-five minutes in total, and afterwards the boy joined Adam inside one of the cannabis clubs buried deep within an alleyway on Venice Beach Boulevard.

The boy stepped into the cool air-conditioned front room that was illuminated only by blacklights. After taking a couple steps into the foyer, the boy stood in front of a ticket-window. Behind the window a man sat staring into a computer screen. As the boy approached the counter the man lazily looked up with a glazed look in his eyes. "How stereotypical." The boy thought, that the receptionist at a cannabis club would be high as a kite. The man leaned forward into a microphone.

"New patient?" He inquired with a much softer voice than the boy had expected from the big man.

"Yeah, I have my card right here." The boy replied into a few black slits in the glass which he assumed was a microphone from his side. As he said this the boy reached into his pocket and pulled the folded up piece of paper from the bottom. After carefully unfolding the recommendation the boy set it inside the ticket drawer, which slid back into the booth. The boy made a mental note to get the piece of paper laminated, as he could see it tearing easily. He then watched as the man examined the recommendation.

After an agonizing minute the man looked up at the boy with a blank stare.

"So you went to Dr. Ruckenfold?"

"Uhh. Yeah." The boy stammered out, unsure of why the man was questioning his brand new recommendation, fresh out of the printer.

"Right down the beach there? Yeah we don't accept new patients from him, cocksucker's been writing fake recs for years."

The boy stared in astonishment at the man, he didn't know what to say, and the man seemed completely serious in his accusation of the doctor. The man seemed to notice the blank stare the boy gave back to him, and cracked a smile which turned into a full-bellied laugh.

"I'm just fucking with you! I gotta do that to all new patients, let me see your ID real quick homie, gotta make sure you're you." The man said to the boy.

Deciding to go along with the man's good-natured joke, the boy joined in the laughter. After passing under his ID and getting the two documents back, the man explained a few rules of the club. They were mostly common sense, no heckling the bud-tenders, no phones out in the back room, and if you were staying and smoking you needed to leave your ID and keys with the receptionist.

The boy agreed to the rules and handed the man his car keys and ID. The man stepped out of the ticket booth for a moment only to reappear through a side door the boy hadn't previously noticed under the black lights. The boy stepped past the man into a well-lit hallway, there the man took the boy's photo and took down some general information about him to build a patient history.

Finally the man handed the boy a simple blue ticket (like the ride tickets found at carnivals) and pointed him further down the hallway towards another door. The boy cooly walked down the hallway, anticipation running through his veins as he came closer to finally seeing what lay behind the locked doors of cannabis clubs. As he pushed open the door he came to the revelation that his expectations were set a little bit too high. The "cannabis club" was essentially a hookah lounge, with assorted couches and coffee tables that seemed to be found outside of different garage sales in different states of disrepair. Along the back wall was a bar with stools and scales, and behind the bar were the bud tenders and shelves upon shelves of mason jars filled with nugs and labeled by name and type of weed.

Further down the shelves were boxes of prerolled joints, blunts, edibles, and wax. The boy found Adam perched on a barstool talking to a handsome bud tender in a tight white Tee with the club logo on it and clean cut hair. Adam had a type, that was for certain. The boy sat down next to his friend with a proud smile.

"Hey! Jakey welcome to the party room!" Adam said with an exuberant smile. He then gave the bud tender behind the bar a flirty smile and asked him to bring the boy their daily new-patient deal. Staring up at the rows of weed the boy had no idea where to begin, so he nodded his approval towards the bud tender and watched as the man walked behind the shelves and out of sight.

"So, do you know him or is this you trying to pick up the bartender? Which usually doesn't work out well just so you know." The boy said as he turned to his friend.

Adam flushed a bright red and turned to check if the bud tender had returned yet. "Well I strolled in and saw a pretty face, of course I'm going to try and chat him up."

"You are such a man-whore. It's disgusting really." The boy replied uneasily as he stared at the kid in front of him.

"Not my fault you chose monogamy over the playboy lifestyle. You could be enjoying all the fruits this beautiful world has to offer, but no. you took the first fruit that fell into your lap."

"Jesus Christ Adam, tell me how you really feel." The boy groaned and sunk down onto his elbows on the bar in front of him. He knew just how easy it would be for him to go to parties and hook up with a different girl every weekend. But there was still something that yearned inside of him for something more. He felt the difference between Amanda and Jfer. Sex with Amanda had been drunk, sloppy, and half-hazard. Sex with his girlfriend was passionate, emotional, and all-in-all more satisfying.

As his head spun the bud tender returned with a gift basket in one hand and an oil rig in the other. Upon reaching the two boys the man reached out his hand to introduce himself as Rashad. The boy hadn't noticed it initially, but the man did have a sun-kissed pigment that in fact wasn't from tanning like the boy thought, but genes.

Rashad pulled each item out of the basket, starting with an eighth of top shelf weed for thirty-five, a triple-dose chocolate bar for fifteen, two prerolled joints for ten, and a gram of wax for fifty. All in all it was a gift basket valued at just over a hundred dollars, but for first time patients the basket came with a free dab on the house and was offered at the low-low price of only ninety dollars. The boy knew it was a solid deal, so he took Rashad up on the gift basket and was soon presented with a fat glob of wax. While the Bud tender flexed his muscles and held a blow torch over the nail, Adam chatted him up, asking simple questions like how long he had worked at the club, if he was from socal, and if he went to school in the area. Rashad was courteous in his responses, but the boy could tell from the glances he shot down the bar that Adam was not his type.

The man was currently eyeing down a bleach blonde with a tank top covering her bikini top, she was struggling with the process of sliding on the tiny shorts she had procured from her friends grey backpack. Everyone in the room was low-key shooting glances as the girl continued to play the ditz card. The boy regarded the spectacle as quiet possibly the most desperate cry for attention he had seen in a while.

Adam seemed to catch on to the sudden shift in focus of the room, and groaned when he saw the object of people's fixation. The girl was clearly too high for her own good and was making a fool of herself giggling and geeking out over trying to squeeze her muffin top into the waistband of her denims.

Rashad snapped to his senses at some point and pulled the torch off the nail. The boy waited a moment for the titanium to cool slightly before pressing the wax down against it and inhaling. Once the wax had completely melted off of the sharp edge of one side the boy flipped the tool and cold-capped the rig, releasing a jet of smoke that accelerated through the twisting glass pipe with its percolators and water-filters. After completely clearing all the smoke from the glass the boy set the tool down on the bar next to the rig and sat back in the bar stool, allowing his mind off the leash.

The first to come was the wracking cough. The boy rarely coughed when it came to weed, but dabs tickled his lungs in a way that forced him to cough and gasp for air. Soon he began to feel light-headed, which was quickly replaced by the dull throbbing of the dab taking its toll on the boy's sobriety.

The two teens remained at the club for about an hour before the boy finally pulled Adam away from the bud tender. With gift basket in hand the boy returned to the front desk and retrieved his ID and keys, saying goodbye to the receptionist who had literally opened the door to medicinal marijuana for the boy.

Stepping into the afternoon sunlight forced the boys to put their sunglasses on. The duo walked along the streets of Venice until they reached the challenger. Adam didn't need much convincing to take the trip up to Santa Monica with the boy, and despite not being privy to the reason for their journey, he went along with it in his usual optimistic fashion.

The tattoo shop was only a ten-minute drive from where they had been parked, but upon realizing where it was in relativity to the Santa Monica Pier, the boy wondered if they might have saved time by keeping their parking spot. Luckily there was one open spot that had been left only a stone's throw away from the shop. As the boy stepped out of his car and began to lead the way towards the hole-in-the-wall tattoo parlor, his anticipation began to build. The day had finally come, he was going to permanently mark up his body in a form of self-expression and freedom.

Of course all the boy could think about at the moment was Natalie, and the swirl of emotions that flooded his head every time his mind conjured up an image of her. It was almost four-thirty and the mid-day crowds were starting to look haggard and worn-thin from a day in the sun. Adam followed the boy as he confidently weaved through the crowds until he reached the storefront he was looking for.

Flaming Dragon Tattoo looked like something out of an eighties movie. Even the outdated pictures out front depicted men with mullets showing off their new artwork. Adam finally caught on to what the boy was doing and let out a yelp of excitement.

"YOU'RE GETTING A TATTOO?!" He asked excitedly as the boy turned to face him with a grin.

"I'm just going to get a quote on a tattoo. If I like the design and it's a decent price I'll consider getting it done today. No guarantees that I'm walking out of here with a tattoo today Adam." The boy tried to contain his own excitement. He knew exactly what he wanted and he knew that he would be getting the tattoo that day.

"You're getting a tattoo, I won't let you leave without one. Wait until Jfer hears about this." As he said this Adam pulled his phone out of his pocket and began frantically trying to enter his password while fighting off the sun's intense glare.

"No! This is going to be a surprise, no Snapchat story, no group text, nobody is to know until we get back to the house. Deal?"

Adam seemed irritated but he begrudgingly accepted the boy's terms. With that taken care of the boy opened the door to the shop and stepped inside.

Chapter 21

The boy stepped into a dusty barber-shop style building, with a front desk followed by multiple booths behind it. In one of the booths there was a large Hispanic artist working on a young woman's forearm. He was carefully aiming his instrument around the edge of a rose petal, the effortlessness with which he maneuvered the small needle made the perfect curve even more impressive.

The girl sitting in the chair getting the tattoo was looking down at the artist's needle, she had a look of enthrallment and pride. The petal was part of an elaborate corsage of red and yellow roses that wrapped around her wrist. as the boys eyes traced up the woman's arm he observed how the top of the corsage morphed into the tail of a scorpion, which covered most of the skin surrounding her elbow and lower bicep. Above this was a pattern of swirls and shading that reminded the boy of Chinese paintings of water. At the top of her arm was a lighthouse that stretched to the end of her shoulder.

"How you guys doing today?" The high-pitched voice snapped the boy out of his gaze. Natalie was the definition of stunning, and her tattoos was perhaps the cherry on top- that which separated her from typical "hot girls".

The boy turned to the person working the front desk, expecting a dainty young woman based off the high-pitched voice. Instead he was confronted by a greying man rocking a three-day old beard, faded blue jeans, a stained T-shirt, and a body that suggested at least a collegiate athlete career, or time in the armed forces. Both of the man's arms were covered in sleeve tattoos and he had a neckpiece which appeared to lead down underneath his Tee. The boy was caught off guard, and the moment of awkward silence seemed to catch the attention of the woman in the seat.

"Look who showed up." Natalie said in a cool tone, flashing the boy a look that could make nations go to war. The fact that he was still pretty high gave him a light confidence.

"I figured I couldn't miss an opportunity to let you dig a needle into my skin" The boy replied back. Light confidence, but not a lot of suave.

The girl giggled in response. "Well check in with Steve and I'll be with you in a minute." She then smiled at the boy before turning her attention to Adam, who was darting his eyes suspiciously between the boy and Natalie.

"Oh this is Adam by the way, he came in today for emotional support."

The other boy seemed to loosen up upon hearing his name, and introduced himself as the boy's lover. This elicited another fit of giggles from the woman in the chair.

The boy narrowed his eyes and shook his head at Natalie, insinuating the ridiculousness of his friend's claim. He then turned back to the man at the desk, finally acknowledging his presence.

"Steve I assume?"

The man cracked a smile, and offered his hand for the boy to shake.

"Jake Rivera. Good to meet you." The boy said as he took the man's hand in his own. His skin was silky smooth, which again caught the boy off guard. He was expecting a calloused and rough man's hand.

Adam stepped up on his own at this point, smiling and introducing himself as he cut in front of the boy. The man didn't seem to notice, and instead took Adam's hand in his own. Their eyes met for a split second and a look crossed both of their faces. The boy played it off as if he hadn't noticed, but he knew Adam was already planning his pickup of the older man who broke the silence.

"So which one of you handsome young gents is here for Natalie's four-thirty?"

Adam tested the waters with his response.

"Well Jake is here for Natalie, but if you're available I might just have to lay down on one of those tables as well."

The man let out a booming laugh that didn't match up with his voice.

"Unfortunately kid someone has to man the front desk." Adam visually cringed at the word 'kid'.

"Oh, about that, here you go." The boy said as he pulled his wallet out and handed his ID across the desk to the man. Adam quickly regained his composure and did the same.

Steve took the boy's ID but slid Adam's back to him.

"Just need the client's ID." The man muttered as he closely examined the boy's license.

"Is he legal?" Natalie chirped from her seat, sliding a wink in the boy's direction.

"Yep, and he's a Taurus, perfect for a slutty scorpio like you." The man said as he turned to shoot a smirk at the girl. Natalie responded with a smile and met eyes with the boy once more before looking back down at the needle dancing across her wrist.

Steve reached into a drawer behind him and pulled a clipboard and pen out. He then set the boy's ID on top of the clipboard and passed it over the desk to him.

"Fill this out, and just so you know we close in three hours, so if it's going to take longer than that you'll have to schedule another appointment."

"Alright sounds good, thanks." The boy replied as he took the clipboard from the man and took a seat in one of the office chairs that lined the back wall, looking into the tattoo booths.

Adam took the seat directly opposite the receptionist, and started up a light conversation with the man. The boy sat on Adam's right, which unintentionally gave him a direct view of Natalie's backside, as she was facing the opposite wall.

The first page on the clipboard asked for basic personal info, his tattoo idea and placement, and the general price cap he was willing to pay. The boy knew he'd be dropping some serious bills on his tattoo regardless, so after checking the balance in his bank account on his phone, he decided to give himself a seven hundred dollar limit.

The combination of his birthday and graduation had helped generate a significant amount of cash for the boy. His parents alone had given him five hundred dollars in spending money. The boy had felt weird accepting the money, it was like his parents were trying to compensate for the fact that the cheating incident had blown over within a couple days.

Mr. Rivera had been understanding of his mother's indiscretion, and agreed to be a more "loving, caring, and passionate" husband.

The second page was a simple liability waiver, which the boy completed with a few of his autographs. The entire process should've taken only a couple minutes, but the boy was distracted-- to say the least-- by the woman in front of him. Whenever the boy would draw a blank his gaze would slowly shift upwards from the paper, only to be entranced by the body of the goddess in front of him. Natalie caught the boy's wandering eyes a few times in the mirror, but would only laugh quietly to herself before returning her gaze to the artist and his needle.

When he had finally completed both forms the boy interrupted Adam's flirting to give the man at the desk the clipboard.

Steve took the board from the boy and began tapping into his keyboard, occasionally looking back at the clipboard to ensure accurate copying. The boy stood awkwardly for a moment before Natalie called out to him. Upon turning to face the girl he saw that she was now standing in front of the chair she had previously been sitting on.

"So I drew up a couple examples of what you asked for. Come check em' out." The woman said as she signaled him to follow her to a booth further down in the shop.

"So, why wings?" Natalie asked back to the boy, keeping the conversation professional. The boy detected a hint of personal interest coming from the woman though as she stopped at the second to last booth in the shop.

"Now what are they doing keeping the prettiest artist all the way in the back? You're their money-maker!" The boy stated with a cocky grin.

"Oh don't worry we have Steve up at the front to be our good-looking first face." Natalie replied back sarcastically.

"Oh yeah about him." The boy said in a hushed tone as he leaned in towards Natalie. "Is he... you know... gay?"

Natalie shiftily looked around the room, pretending to be on the lookout for people that might overhear their quiet whispers. She then leaned in close enough that the boy could smell the perfume emanating off of her.

"No. He's actually a scientologist." The woman whispered excitedly.

"Wait what?" The boy replied in confusion.

"Of course he's gay, dumbass." Natalie said with a satisfied look on her face. "What about that lover of yours? He seems pretty interested in my main man over there."

"Adam?" The boy asked as he looked back at his friend. Adam had gotten up to lean on the counter that encompassed the top of the desk, and was clearly in full-on flirting mode. He was enthusiastically explaining something to Steve and was wildly waving his hands around and laughing throughout his monologue. Steve was laughing and seemed to enjoy the conversation he was having with Adam.

"Oh yeah he's about as straight as a rainbow." The boy explained with a chuckle.

"And you?" Natalie inquired with a playful look in her eye.

"Well I was gay when I walked in, but you're making me feel like I have a choice." The boy replied, returning what he thought was flirting.

The woman had nothing to say and instead held an intense moment of eye-contact with the boy before turning her attention to the binder sitting on the counter behind her.

The boy was still for a moment, shocked a little by the eye-fucking Natalie had just given him.

"So here's a couple different styles and sizes I sketched out." The woman said, pulling him away from the arousing thoughts that swirled through his head. The boy took the small stack of papers the woman held out to him and plopped down into the comfortable leather seat.

After flipping through the designs a few times, the boy decided on one that stretched from shoulder to shoulder. Between the wings was his family crest, a simple shield with two solid blue lines running diagonally across the front. The crest had been passed down through his mother's side of the family for over 200 years. Considering he had inherited his father's name for life, he figured it was only fair to get a symbol of his mother's side permanently attached to him as well.

Natalie kicked a lever under the seat which dropped the boy back towards the floor. The sudden drop forced a quick intake of breath from the boy. Sensing the surprise, Natalie stroked the boy's shoulder and encouraged him to relax.

The boy picked himself up off the back of the chair to pull his shirt off. Now shirtless, he silently thanked his genetics for the toned body he hadn't worked a day in his life for.

"Want me to do some shading on that six pack for you as well? Those bottom two abs could use a little help it looks like." Natalie joked.

"Look all you want hun, but my pimp says you have to pay for anything below the first four." The boy shot back with sass. The woman laughed harder than before, and reached down to steady herself. The boy was unsure if she had purposefully felt his abs or if it was just where her hands had landed. After collecting herself Natalie seemed to notice the placement of her hand on the boy's shirtless torso.

The woman quickly lifted her hand and flushed with embarrassment.

"It's fine, you'll have your hands all over me in a minute anyways." The boy said with a smug grin in an attempt to relieve the momentary awkwardness.

"I'm sorry, I thought you knew I have a boyfriend." Natalie shot back teasingly.

"I thought you knew you had a boyfriend. I meant you'll be tattooing me." The boy declared, putting Natalie back on the defensive.

This time the woman blushed such a dark shade of red she had to turn away from the boy and begin setting up her instrument. The boy watched in silence as the woman went about preparing a tray with paper towels, disinfectant wipes, the tattoo gun, and a vial of ink.

After Natalie applied the three separate stencils to the boy's chest, the outline of his tattoo was formed. The boy sat up for a minute to catch one last glimpse of his bare chest. As he studied the outline of the tattoo, any lingering doubts about his decision vanished. He was getting it, and he was getting it done now.

"Alright. Let's do it." The boy said as he took a deep breath and laid back in the chair.

"Right here? With everyone watching?" Natalie protested.

"You have a dirty mind. I like you." The boy said with a sly grin.

"You keep up kid, I like that." The woman replied. "Okay, so I'm going to start with the crest on your sternum. It'll be the most painful part considering it's right over the bone, let me know if you need a break." She continued.

"Mama didn't raise no bitch." The boy stated confidently.

Natalie pulled a seat up next to the boy and sat down, picking the tattoo gun up off the tray. As she flicked the tiny machine on, a buzzing sound began to resonate from the rapidly moving needle. Placing one hand on the boy's chest, the woman met eyes with the boy one final time and gave him a smile of encouragement, revealing sparkling white teeth.

Chapter 22

The boy was getting antsy. He had spent the past three hours laying back with a needle taking its toll on his chest. The crest had been painful, as Natalie had predicted, but after three hours the pain of the needle was merely an annoyance compared to the pain caused by the paper towels.

Every couple of strokes made by the artist required her to take a paper towel and rub the new ink. Since each stroke applied less than a centimeter of ink, the constant rubbing of the paper towels had caused the boy's skin to become raw and red. Natalie finally finished the outline of the wings and feathers, so the boy proposed a cigarette break.

"I thought Mama didn't raise no bitch?" The woman asked challengingly.

"She didn't, she raised a chain-smoker." The boy replied defensively.

Natalie laughed in response, and agreed that a five-minute cigarette break would be perfect considering her hand had started to cramp up. The boy sat up and admired the piece of art in the mirror. While there wasn't any shading or color yet, the tattoo already looked better than the boy was expecting. It was a work in progress, but progress was going well.

Adam had convinced Steve to join him for a bite to eat on the man's lunch (Dinner) break, so Natalie's coworker Josh had taken over the front desk and was now staring blankly into his phone. After standing and throwing his tank top over his shoulder, the boy started towards the front door. Natalie stopped the boy silently by grabbing his wrist and pulling him back towards her.

"We can go up to the roof if you want? Nice view of the sunset up there." She offered with an innocent look on her face. The boy turned and slid his hand into hers, gesturing for her to show him the way. Natalie smiled and called across the shop to Josh.

"We're going up for a smoke break Josh, text me if you need help finding the 'create new appointment' button."

The man in the desk casually tossed a middle finger in the direction of Natalie, continuing to stare at his phone. The boy chuckled and turned to follow the woman as she led him by a hand out the back door to a set of stairs. The staircase looked older than the building itself, and appeared to once have been painted green. The only remaining signs of paint were a few patches dispersed across the worn brown wood.

The boy followed Natalie up the stairs, and upon reaching the top found himself overlooking the Santa Monica shoreline. The sun had dipped below the waterline minutes before they had come outside, but its light still reached up from the water towards the heavens, painting the sky orange, blue, and every shade of color in between.

"Pretty nice spot huh?" Natalie asked as she pulled the boy down next to her on one of the many couches that surrounded a small fire pit in the middle of the rooftop lounge.

"Yeah, it's beautiful up here." The boy replied, taking caution not to sit too close to the woman. The boy knew he was already pushing his luck by flirting with the girl. The last thing he wanted to do was let his newfound confidence push him to make a move that ended in rejection—or worse—an actual hookup.

Natalie, however didn't seem to care much for the consequences as she swung her legs onto the boys lap and stretched out on the secondhand piece of furniture. Not sure of where to put his hands the boy stretched one arm out across the back of the sofa in the direction of the woman, and let the other rest on the arm of the couch. As he stretched the raw and irritated skin to reach the back of the couch, he realized just how painful it would be to keep his arm up in that position for any period of time longer than a few minutes.

"You should put your arm down, stretching the skin like that can fuck with the fresh ink if you aren't careful." Natalie stated after noticing the boy's obvious discomfort.

"Well you kinda took up all the space on the couch so-" The boy was interrupted as Natalie reached up and took his hand from the back of the couch cushions, placing it gently on her inner thigh. The boy's hand was dangerously close to the cheating zone, so he wordlessly pulled it back to take the pack of cigarettes and lighter out of his pocket. The woman beside him made a huffing sound before politely asking for a cigarette. The boy handed her one, and placed his own to his lips and lit it. Before he knew it, the woman had pulled herself up onto her knees and was leaning forward with the stoag in her mouth.

As he lit the cigarette that hung loosely from the woman's mouth, he tried to avoid making eye contact. Of course the only other things for him to look at were the woman's breasts that struggled to squeeze into her tiny top. Noticing where the boy's gaze had turned, Natalie pulled back from the tiny flame and turned to sit straight-forward in the couch. After a few drags on the cigarette the woman crossed her arms, pushing her boobs up even higher.

"So how's Mr. Jensen doing?" The boy asked in a desperate attempt to remind the woman that what she was doing was wrong.

"He's fine." Natalie stated curtly before taking a drag of her cig.

"That's good." The boy responded, unsure of what to say next to keep the conversation going.

The two sat in silence for a couple minutes, each dragging on their own cigarette and looking out at the rapidly diminishing sunlight. As her cigarette neared its end Natalie rested her head on the boy's shoulder without saying a word. The boy smiled in spite of the situation. A year ago he wouldn't have had the balls to talk to a woman as gorgeous as Natalie. Now here he was on a roof watching the sun set with Helen of Troy trying to tempt him.

The boy knew it was wrong to cheat. He had felt the pain of cheating in his own life already, and now it was his turn to be tempted. The boy was adamant that he could make it through this challenge. He loved Jfer, and wanted nothing or nobody to come between them. Yet as he shot a sideways glance at Natalie resting against his shoulder, the very blood in his veins began to boil with sexual excitement. He couldn't take the temptation for even a second more, and forced himself to stand up.

"Hey, you okay?" The woman asked shyly as the boy took a few steps away from the couch.

"No, no I'm not okay Natalie. I'm pretty fucking far from okay to be honest with you." The boy answered back. He took a few deep breaths in an attempt to calm himself, but was quickly thrown back into the fire as a set of hands wrapped around the boy's waist and pulled him back. Natalie's body was pressed firmly against his back and he could feel the calm and steady breathing of the woman as it tickled the hairs on the back of his neck.

"What's wrong?" Natalie inquired. The tickling of her breath on the boy's neck soon became the soft sensation of lips being pressed against his skin.

"This is what's wrong Natalie!" The boy let out, unable to control the outburst. He pushed himself out of the woman's warm embrace and walked to the edge of the rooftop. There he stood, struggling to control the treachery of what his impulses told him to do. "I have a girlfriend, and you have a boyfriend. A boyfriend who just so happens to have been my high school math teacher. Natalie you're absolutely fucking beautiful and every fiber of my being is telling me to bend you over that couch right now, but doesn't this situation just feel wrong to you?"

There was a pause. The boy took one final drag of his cigarette and flicked it out onto the street below before the woman responded.

"Alex and I are on a break. He's been distant lately and I know I'm going to lose him. I'm sorry Jake."

The boy's mind went blank. There were no thoughts of Jfer, no thoughts of the repercussions, no memory of what his mother had done just weeks before. All that the boy understood was that the woman in front of him considered herself fair game. At long last, his instincts kicked in.

With no intention of moving his feet he was walking towards the woman. He was transfixed by the lost-puppy look in her eyes. He had felt rejection before, and didn't believe anybody else should be forced to go through it. He saw the pain in her eyes and he wanted to help. With no intention of kissing the woman the boy was kissing her.

The kisses were not passionate nor loving like the ones he shared with Jfer (not that the girl was on the boys mind at the time anyways). They were also different from the sloppy face-sucking he had done with Amanda. Kissing Natalie was powerful, nearly electrifying. As she wrapped her hands around the back of the boy's neck, he lifted her off the ground and into his arms. Natalie wrapped her legs around the boys waist and used them to squeeze the two even more tightly together.

Natalie soon began to run her hands through the boy's hair, pulling and playing with it as she kissed him. The boy decided he didn't care anymore. He didn't care if it would take two appointments to get his tattoo done, he didn't care if Adam walked upstairs and discovered what was going on, and he damn sure didn't care if Jfer found out. The blood was pumping and he had one thing in mind- sex.

The boy carried Natalie to the couch and laid her down on her back, soon he was pulling down the skin-tight spandex the woman had on. Finding no resistance up until that point, he moved his lips down the woman's neck, sucking on the sweet skin just hard enough to arouse without leaving trashy hickies all over. Just as he began to pull at Natalie's lace panties, the woman lurched off of her back and pushed him down onto the couch instead.

The boy was pinned down by a firm hand pressing against his chest just under the newly-tattooed skin. He watched as Natalie threw her hair back and seductively straddled him before cupping his stubble-covered face in her hands and kissing him feverishly. The woman then slipped her hand inside the waistband of the boy's board shorts.

Things accelerated quickly at this point. Natalie's natural beauty and the way she could move her hips forced things to be end quicker than the boy had hoped for, but he knew there would be another chance for him to prove his endurance to the woman. The sex was synchronized, as if their two bodies had been made for each other. Even though it had been quick, both participants had been satisfied, and when it was over there was silence.

The two put their clothes on before sitting back down on the couch and looking out at the last few traces of light blue sky on the edge of the horizon. Words were incapable of describing how the two felt, so instead of talking, or joking, or trying to rationalize what they had just done, they would simply turn and look at each other, with mutual feelings of admiration. Finally Natalie broke the silence.

"Alrighty. Well. We've been up here for thirty minutes, I think that's getting close to enough time for Josh to find a way to burn down the building. Let's head down so I can get back to work on you."

"Yeah I'm sure Adam will be back any minute with Steve and I'd rather he didn't know about what we just did." The boy replied. As the words left his mouth he realized the horror of his actions.

He had cheated. He had fucked Natalie. He had a girlfriend. He had cheated on his girlfriend. The boy's stomach began to tie itself into knots as his mind continuously repeated the four statements over and over.

"We should uh… Definitely do that again though. You're not too bad." Natalie murmured quietly.

"Not too bad? That's not how you felt a couple minutes ago." The boy replied smugly. Why was he still flirting?

"Well you did cut me off after one quick hit, what's a girl supposed to do?" She fired back.

"Natalie I'm not a drug you want to get hooked on. I have a girlfriend, and I'm leaving in two months for college across the country." The boy said reluctantly. He had screwed up already, but hopefully this was his chance to fix things, by never letting it happen again.

The woman stared at the boy for a second whilst thinking of a comeback. Instead of saying anything she sat back down on the boy's lap, wrapping her legs around his waist and running her fingernails along his back.

"You see the thing is darling, I don't get addicted to drugs." Suddenly her nails dug into the boy's back, causing him to sit up in sharp pain. She then leaned into his ear and whispered "I just enjoy the shit out of them while I can."

With that Natalie rose to her feet and left the boy sitting on the couch alone with his thoughts and a half-chub.

Chapter 23

The boy walked to the banister on the side of the building, his head was spinning and his stomach turning. As he reached the edge he heaved his body forward. Half an attempt to throw himself off for the atrocity he had committed, and half to help pump the vomit that protested to be released.

What had he done? His vision was blotchy and the pain in his abdomen and chest was forcing his entire face to cringe. Blinking away tears, the boy's vision finally cleared, revealing a sight that nearly made him heave again. There, in the alley beside the tattoo shop, tucked against the shadowed wall, stood Adam and Steve. The two looked up at the boy with a look of disgust and shock.

The boy wiped his mouth and fired a glob of spit into the alleyway in front of the two figures who were now trying to casually step apart. The boy threw his head in the air and took a deep breath. The nausea was gone, but his nerves had hardly settled. Adam's presence throughout his embarrassing display over the balcony forced the boy's mind to run circles. How the hell was he supposed to explain this?

They had enjoyed a few beers before the dab bar, so the boy figured that was his best chance at a halfway-decent cover-up. After taking another deep breath, the boy looked down into the alley and let out a nervous laugh.

"What's up guys?"

With no intention of doing so, the boy put Adam on the defensive.

"Umm, nothing. Just. You knowww." His friend called back up to the boy. He had an embarrassed look on his face and his eyes couldn't stop darting between the boy on the roof and the man standing next to him.

Finally coming to his senses, the boy realized that his projectile vomit had rudely cock-blocked his friend below.

"Oh God you two weren't..." The boy began, a look of comic disgust on his face.

"DON'T make this a gay thing, *Jake*." Adam said pointedly.

"It's not a gay thing dumbass, you just met him!" Replied the boy, offended that Adam had mistaken his pointed humor for bigotry.

"Oh, so did you already know the tattoo chick then? Is that why she's okay to fuck?" Adam fired back. Even in the shadows the boy could see the look of disapproval on his friends face.

"What the fuck are you talking about?" The boy responded defensively.

Up until now, Steve had been awkwardly standing to Adam's right, concealed by a heavier darkness brought on by the shadow of the building. Silently he stepped further out of the shadows so the boy could see him clearly.

"You think you're the first one she's brought up to that couch, kid?" The man asked.

Speechless, and with the urge to wretch once more twisting his insides, the boy turned away from the balcony and began striding toward the stairs. The calls of Adam and Steve hardly registered. The boy needed to leave the horrible house of sin that he had earlier been so excited to visit.

As his foot landed on the first step leading down, a gut-retching realization struck the boy, causing his knee to wobble unsupported, and hand to shoot out for the rail. How the fuck did he expect to leave the parlor behind when he had an unfinished tattoo sitting on his chest? The boy looked down at the raw skin and fresh ink and was disturbed. The tattoo would forever be a reminder of what he had done today.

His family crest was the only part of the tattoo that had been completed. The boy found it ironic that he had adorned the symbol of his mother's heritage while cheating on his beloved. The apple didn't fall far from the tree, the boy supposed.

Realizing that he had only made it down one step, the boy snapped to his senses. He took two deep breaths to steady his legs, and began to walk down the stairs. He had no plan for what was to come, but figured no matter how he tried to explain the situation,

Adam was most assuredly going to tell Jfer. There was no escaping his punishment. The girl would find out.

Struggling to resist the downward and negative spiral of his thoughts, the boy knew of only one remedy that could help him and it was sitting in a gift basket in the car. As he attempted to casually stroll into the tattoo shop, his expression of anxious disbelief gave him away immediately.

"Alright, so do you want to pay me for overtime or come back later?" Came a voice from beside him. The boy—startled by the voice—snapped out of the haze that had taken over his mind and senses.

"No. No I'm done with you." He replied, unable to look at the woman who had snapped his streak of self-righteousness.

"Excuse me?" Natalie replied with a nervous laugh. The boy turned to see a look of incredulity on her face.

"I'm done with you. You pushed my boundaries and now I did something that I'll carry with me forever. Don't you understand how much of a fucked up person you are? You're actively going out and breaking the rules of your commitment!" The boy was getting worked up, and his temper was beginning to show.

The woman could tell she had gotten a rise out of the boy, and in order to further antagonize him replied in a smooth voice of silk, "It takes two to tango honey. But if you say so then that's fine. You can find another artist to finish your tattoo. Oh wait, every artists style is unique, which means those are going to turn out looking like shit." She stated with sass as she pointed to the boys half-finished tattoo.

"I don't care, I hate this tattoo now. Every time I look at it I'll be forced to remember how I fucked the worthless slut that put it on me." Just as he was saying this, the door opened and Adam and Steve started in. Who upon realizing the situation of conflict, quietly ducked back outside.

Natalie had been offended by the boy's choice of words and decided to put him in his place. "Listen here you little shit." She began, with the tone of a mother who just found out her twelve-year old child had been kicked out of school for disrupting class.

"You think you've got it all figured out because you're eighteen, have a girlfriend that loves you, and a daddy who buys you whatever you want. Well wake up kid. The real world isn't fucking catered to you. You make choices, you get hit in the face with the consequences. I've learned to become comfortable with some consequences, but you clearly haven't. Just because you cheated on your girlfriend you think your whole world is ending. Guess what? It's not that big of a deal! You live and you learn! You can do better than her!"

"Shut up." The boy interjected forcefully. His hands were trembling. He knew if she kept digging he wouldn't be able to control his anger.

"I'm splitting up with Alex, so now I have to find a new place to live! That's real, Jake. That's an adult consequence. You should be honored I decided to pursue an awkward gangly little shit like you."

The boy had had enough. He didn't know how much the tattoo was worth unfinished, but he didn't feel as though the witch beside him deserved much of a tip. He pulled three hundred dollars out of his wallet and slowly walked towards the woman. As he got closer a strange look passed over the woman- was it fear? The boy disregarded the look and stopped an inch away from Natalie's face.

"You sicken me. I'm an eighteen year-old kid that you took advantage of. You think you've gotten it all figured out because you can hurt people and not feel anything. Your heart is cold and you leave misery in your wake. Do not lecture me like a child when I know the only reason you allow yourself to hurt is because you've been hurt before. I'm better than you. I'll fix what I did wrong. You on the other hand, you'll be forced to ruin one good thing after another until you find yourself alone in life." The boy took the moment of silence to gently place the three-hundred dollars in the displaced bra strap of the artist.

"Thank you for your work, but I don't think I'm going to leave a tip today." And with that the boy turned and marched out of the tattoo shop, angrily slamming through the door on his way out.

He was halfway to the car when Adam finally caught up to him.

"Jake!" He exclaimed before cutting his sprint to a fast-paced walk to match the boy's.

The boy said nothing in response to his friend, and instead began the arduous process of putting his tank-top back on without irritating or getting it stuck to the new ink that covered his chest.

"Shit man you should've at least gotten that wrapped or covered or something, it could get infected like that." Adam offered sheepishly.

"I don't FUCKING CARE about the tattoo Adam!" The boy furiously let out. He hadn't meant to snap on his friend, but the explosion was a long-time coming, Adam had been the unfortunate bystander who had to take the heat.

"I don't FUCKING care about that bitch, about this tattoo, about your new fuckbuddy Steve, I just don't care. I want to be here anymore man come on." They had finally arrived at the challenger, so between the tears that obscured the boy's vision, he opened the back seat and tore through the gift basket. Upon finding the edible he was looking for, the boy unwrapped it and popped the whole thing in his mouth.

Adam made his way into the passenger seat of the car and quietly sat down, folding his arms across his chest. Once the boy had taken his seat on the driver's side and started the car, Adam proceeded to pull the pack of cigarettes from his pocket.

"Hot and ready, get 'em while they're free." The friend stated emotionlessly as he held up a cigarette for the boy.

Without saying a word the boy took one of the cigarettes and placed it in his mouth. As he lit up the end hanging away from his lips, his friend rolled down the windows on-queue. They sat in silence for a moment, the boy focused on getting as far away from the tattoo shop as fast as possible. Adam on the other side was staring out the window, admiring the view of the now moonlit beach.

It was a simple maneuver, just a slight bend in the road, leading to a tunnel. The boy looked to his friend and thought about how sorry he was for turning on him. Adam hadn't deserved the focus of his anger. He had simply been there.

"Adam, you know I care. And I'm not m-" And the boy's words were swallowed by a sharp intake of breath as the car lifted over the curb and launched into the dark night.

Chapter 24

The boy awoke to the smell of clean-washed linens and lemon scented antibacterial scrub. The shit must have been industrial strength, because it overpowered the boy's senses until he saw yellow. In an attempt to get a gathering of his surroundings, the boy cracked open his eyes. The blinding luminescence of the lights continued the trend of leaving a glowing image of yellow well after he shut his eyes again.

Something had caught the boy's attention though during the brief glimpse of the outside world. The boy gathered himself and opened his eyes again. The light was breathtaking, and he had to blink several times before his vision cleared up. He was staring at a white stucco ceiling. The intense illumination came from an industrial light mounted to the ceiling just over his left ear.

What had caught the boy's eye had been the hand that dangled over the edge of his bed. The fingers were old and calloused, and a single golden wedding band winked at him. As his vision slowly returned to him the boy looked around. He was in a white room, lying propped up on a standard hospital bed. His left arm was wrapped in a cast, and there was a throbbing pain in his neck. However none of this compared to the pain that wracked his chest, making him wheeze and sputter for breath. The pain came on so quickly the boy felt as if he had gotten the wind knocked out of him.

The gasps for air attracted the attention of the hand that rested over the bed. His father's head poked up next to the boy's. He had a sleepy look in his eyes but when he saw his son struggling for air he leapt into action. As his dad shouted for help the boy's ears were left ringing, but the man slid his hands under the boy and lifted him up a few inches, opening his lungs to expand freely.

After taking a few deep breaths to calm himself the boy watched as a male nurse strolled into the room, confidently taking over for his father. The man introduced himself as Iche— pronounced *itch*—and explained that the boy had hurtled his car off of Pacific Coast Highway twenty feet to a parking lot below. As the car had plummeted downward he had been saved by the angle of their launch. The nurse went into detail telling the boy how the front bumper had taken the majority of the impact instead of the bottom, had they bottomed out evenly on the landing the boy's spine most likely would have shattered. As it was he had broken both bones in the forearm he had been hanging out the window with his cigarette.

The force of the front of the car hitting first had thrown both passengers forward, only to be smashed back by the airbag. While it had saved his life, the impact against the newly-etched tattoo had been what caused the wracking pain the boy felt in his chest. After the boy had regained his breath and had a general understanding of the situation the man called Iche set the boy down gingerly on his back.

"Dad, Adam?" The boy squeaked out between shallow breaths. The two simple words forced his body into a hacking, gut-clenching cough. The boy pulled himself up to spit off the side of the bed. A chunky sample of blood splattered against the linoleum floor.

"Umm is that normal?" The man asked the nurse, a look of concern on his face. The boy stood staring at the red eye-sore that stood out against the plain white backdrop.

The nurse took one look at the ground before turning towards the father, trying to pass his assurance on with a pat on the shoulder.

"He'll be fine, we made sure there was no serious internal bleeding. Jake I'm going to run and get you a bowl, you might have to spit a few more of those up before you're up and around."

The boy wiped his mouth and nodded his agreement to the nurse before resting his head back against the pillow behind him. Iche turned and strode out of the room in search of a sanitary bowl for the patient in his care.

The boy turned to see his father enthusiastically thumbing away on his iPhone. Left without the one answer he needed, the boy tried once more to catch the attention of the man sitting next to him.

"Dad." His voice stronger now, the boy coughed a few more times.

His father finished typing out the text to the boy's mother before slowly, cautiously, setting the phone on his knee. The fact that he was delaying the answer did nothing to quell the boy's nerves.

"Jake. You need to rest up. Your mother, sister, and Jfer are on their way."

"No!" The boy exclaimed in fear, causing another coughing attack. As he struggled to catch his breath the man beside him looked at the boy with sadness.

"Jake. Jake my boy." The man stood up and took a few steps away from the boy lying in the bed. His shoulders tightened and relaxed unnaturally, giving away his own gasping breaths. When his father turned back around the boy saw that he had tears streaming down his face. "Jake." The man said again before quickly closing the distance between himself and the hospital bed and wrapping the boy in a hug.

"I love you son. You must always know that. I love you, and your mother loves you, and your sister loves you, and so many people love you Jake." The boy's breath caught halfway in his chest. Partially from the weight of his father's crushing bear hug and partially from the emotions that rushed into him all at once. The pain of what he had done struck him before the memory of what he had done flashed before his eyes.

Iche interrupted the father-son moment by clearing his throat and setting a cereal-sized bowl next to the boy's bed. The father pulled himself off of the boy, and returned to his perch next to the bed. The boy's head was spinning and pounding under the oncoming emotions—fear, pain, grief, and shame were forcefully thrown from the boy's innards out into the bowl placed beside him. After a few dry-heaves, black spots began to appear in the boy's vision. As he turned to face his father again his head rested against the pillow and his body fell unconscious under the swirl of thoughts and emotions.

His subconscious gave the boy no reprieve, however, and he was forced to relive his actions over, and over. The memory of his indiscretion with Natalie played in his head on repeat like a vine. He remembered the sharp tingle of the needle passing over his skin, the soft touch of Natalie's lips, the look on Adam's face as the car plummeted off the cliff towards the rapidly-approaching ground.

The boy finally awoke once more to a nightmare nearly as terrifying as the one that had met him in his dreams. Though the light didn't hurt his head as much anymore, the face staring back at him forced his breathing to take on a shaky and nervous pant. Jfer was there in front of the boy. Her eyes were red from crying and lack of sleep, but as fresh teardrops began to trickle down her face the girl broke into a smile.

"Jake, you fucking turd." Was all she could say before rushing to the boy's side and embracing him. The boy's breathing rasped in protest, but the girl was kissing him, unaware of the pain she was putting him through. The boy lay still, fully aware of what he had done to his girlfriend, fully aware of the pain he would soon put her through.

There was something in the feverishness with which she kissed the boy. He had been in a car accident and the boy understood that, but the tears of relief that had once glistened against the girl's face quickly began to turn into a distraught sob. Jfer wrapped her arms around the boy's neck and cried into his pillow. As he protectively placed a hand on the back of her head the boy looked forward to see his mother and sister standing in shock.

The boy's sister had a look of grief in her eyes that his mother was poorly trying to disguise in her own. He didn't understand. He was alive? Sure he had scared his loved ones but what was up with the hospital soap opera? And then it hit him. The question knocked the boy senseless. How had he still not gotten an answer?

"Adam." The boy stated simply. Demanding to know what had happened to his friend with one simple word. The reaction he received sucked every emotion out of his body, and he felt himself go cold.

Jfer let out a cry of despair into the pillow, pulling herself even tighter against the boy. His sister ran to the opposite side of the bed and wrapped the boy's head in her arms, he felt the shuddering of her breath against his temple, he felt the soft kisses his sister planted on his head, and he felt the look his mom was giving him from the end of the hospital bed.

And then he felt nothing. He knew. While his worst fears hadn't been confirmed, the boy knew. Adam was dead.

"What happened?" He choked out. His voice sounded muted, as if it had come from somewhere behind him.

His mother couldn't hold herself together for another moment. In a display that would earn her an Oscar, the woman snapped, launching herself towards the boy's bed. There she wrapped herself around the only thing she could- the boy's leg and began to let out a lament unlike any other. The boy could do nothing. He didn't understand.

It was impossible, the boy thought. His friend was not dead. There would be no funeral, no mourning, there would be a walk two rooms down and he would find the other boy with some stitches and a few broken bones, still as stupidly-charming and annoying as ever. Adam couldn't be gone. He couldn't.

And yet, as he lie there, surrounded by those who loved him, he knew. The bodies that hung on to him were not crying purely out of joy that Adam had survived the accident. This was death. This was the old enemy that had not confronted the boy since the loss of his cousin. There, in that sterilized white room, surrounded by people that loved him, the boy felt alone. He felt singled out.

All of a sudden a second wave of emotion swept over the boy. He cried out in anguish and struggled to fight off the affection of the ladies on his bed. They held him down, cooing and reassuring him that everything would be alright. Then he was sobbing, and holding on tightly to Jfer. The girl shared his pain, and their tears fell together for the next hour as the boy fought off guilt, anguish, and fear.

Finally when he had cried himself dry, the boy asked once more to see his father, and asked that everyone except Jfer leave. His sister understood that the boy was distraught, so she kissed him once more on the head, reminded the boy she loved him, and headed for the door, sniffling and wiping at her eyes.

His mother pulled herself off of the boy's feet to give him a kiss on the cheek. She rested a hand against the side of his head and assured him once more that "Everything would be alright" even though the boy knew nothing was alright.

As his mother followed his sister out of the hospital room, she caught her father at the entrance. The man embraced her, and in that moment the boy saw the spark. That spark which he had always associated with love. That spark which he hadn't noticed in his parent's relationship for years. The woman pulled herself away from the man, gave him a kiss, and tried to force a smile before walking out of the boy's vision.

The boy's father then turned towards the two teens sharing the hospital bed. Jfer hadn't lifted her head from the pillow since originally resting it there, but the sound of the man's approaching footsteps caused her to turn and look towards the newest arrival. Upon seeing that it was the patriarch, the girl wiped her eyes and nose and cleared her throat.

"Hi Mr. Rivera. Jake told me to stay, I hope that's okay." The girl said in a hollow and emotionless voice. The boy could feel her heart pounding against his shoulder.

"Hun it's time I spoke to Jake alone. He's going to have a few guests here in a minute and I'd rather have the room to ourselves until they come in." The man replied in an apologetic tone.

Jfer seemed to know what guests the father was talking about, and slowly began to pull herself up and away from the boy.

"No. Dad I need Jfer here. Please. Whatever it is you can tell her too." The boy objected, pulling his girlfriend back to him. The girl cracked a smile and rested her head down on his stomach.

Mr. Rivera, realizing that he was outnumbered, decided Jfer was privy to the information as well.

"Alright, well Jake. I don't know where to start bud." His father took a few more steps, drawing within arms-reach of the boy. He reached out and took hold of the fingers protruding from the cast. The boy would look back on this moment and remember how slowly time seemed to move. Jfer pulling herself tighter against the boy, the man staring down at his son with sadness weighing heavy on his heart.

"Son, Adam is dead." His father stated simply. The boy could tell how hard it was for the man to force out these words.

"And the thing is. You were driving." He paused here to collect himself. "When you arrived at the hospital they did a toxicology report and found high levels of THC in your blood. Jake, they're…"

The man trailed off as the sound of heavy footsteps rapidly approached the room. Two cops entered with serious faces.

"Jacob Rivera?" One of the officers asked. He was a short and stocky Asian man, with a chest that threatened to break the buttons on his shirt, a low-cut hairstyle, and biceps that stretched the sleeves of his uniform to their max. The boy recognized his partner as Officer Jensen. Upon meeting eyes the boy let out a laugh in spite of the situation.

"Of course you'd be the one to show up." He said in an attempt to be upbeat. The officer didn't seem very happy.

"Duty calls Jake. I just wish I never had to see you in this kind of situation." The officer replied in a serious tone. The boy was now worried.

"Mr. Rivera." The shorter of the two officers began, before clarifying. "Jake. I'm sorry, but we need you to walk us through what happened the other night."

"The other night?" The boy asked in shock. "How long has it been?"

"Jake you've been unconscious for two days." Jfer whispered in his ear.

"TWO DAYS?" The boy exclaimed. "Why the fuck didn't anyone wake me up? Why didn't anyone tell me?" And then the renewed thought of his dead friend brought about a second-wind of pain.

"Jake we need you to calm down. What do you remember of the accident? Give us the story from where you were before you got in the car." Officer Jensen replied in a softer tone.

But the boy couldn't speak. He didn't know where to start. Should he explain the situation with Natalie? Why he had driven off so recklessly? Jfer's whimpering body next to his own gave the boy the answer he didn't want.

"I uhh. I came out of the tattoo shop with Adam, and decided to eat the edible I had left in the back seat. Because my chest hurt from the tattoo." The boy figured this was a good enough back story. "I knew it would take about an hour or so for my body to metabolize the THC and get me high, and my phone told me it was about a half-hour drive back to Adam's." His voice cracked as he stumbled over his friend's name. "So I figured I'd be fine. I was about to enter the tunnel on PCH when I turned to see what Adam was looking at out the window. When I did I felt a bump under the car. I remember I thought it was weird, It didn't feel like a pothole. Next thing I know the car is flying off a cliff and I'm looking at my best friend for the last time." As the final words left his lips the boy's gaze drifted away from the officer's face and he felt the sting of new tears being pushed out of the corner of his eyes.

There was a moment of silence. Jfer took the boy's hand in her own for reassurance. Finally the Asian officer spoke up again. This time in a much more understanding and concerned voice. "So you were completely sober the entire car ride?"

"Yes sir." The boy replied in a serious tone. He knew that he was now facing manslaughter. He knew that he could face years in prison for what he done. None of this mattered. The boy knew that he had killed his friend. And as this fact sunk into his soul, the boy reached out for the bowl beside his bed and vomited more blood.

"You and your friend hadn't been drinking at all earlier? Nothing else in your system at the time that might've impaired your judgment?" Officer Jensen inquired with a pointed gaze.

"No sir, we were both completely sober. I was just lucky."

"Luck had nothing to do with it son." His father interjected, exchanging a look with the police officer.

"What do you mean?" The boy asked, feeling left out of the conversation.

"Jake..." His girlfriend started quietly, "Adam didn't have a seatbelt on."

"What?" He replied in disbelief. "No, Adam always put his seatbelt on. He used to bitch at us about not doing it all the time!"

"Adam wasn't wearing his seatbelt Mr. Rivera." The short and serious cop confirmed. When you hit the parking lot he was..." The man paused for a second, choosing his next word carefully, "ejected."

Suddenly an image came to the boy. He wasn't sure if it had been conjured up by his imagination or if he had seen it while slipping in and out of consciousness. Adam was lying face down on the concrete, his neck twisted in an awkward and grotesque angle. There was smoke rising from the hood of the challenger and as the boy drearily blinked and looked around he saw a hole smashed in the front windshield, blood dripping from the sharp glass poking out in every direction.

Then he was crying again. Uncontrollably this time, sobbing into the embrace of his girlfriend. The girl that had been the catalyst for all of the tragedy that had come from the past couple days. The boy cried for Jfer, and the knowledge that he would have to tell her the real reason for Adam's death. He cried for Adam, and the fact that he would never be able to explain his outburst, or apologize. Then he cried for Adam's parents. He had been their only child, and they had adored and loved him like the baby Jesus.

The two officers realized the boy was in no state to answer questions, so they took their leave. Before following his partner, Jensen rested a caring hand on the boy's shoulder.

"It'll be okay kid." The man started. He looked as if he had more to say, but decided against it and instead gave a smile of encouragement and made his departure, trying to catch up to his partner who walked surprisingly fast despite the short and stubby legs that carried him.

The boy's father stayed for a time, and although he had nothing to offer the boy besides a strong hand to hold, this was more than enough to comfort him. After a while the man embraced his son again, and told him he'd return in a couple hours after work. The boy appreciated the fact that his father had stayed as long as he could, and thanked him. Before making his leave, the man asked if Jfer wanted a ride home. The girl let out a muffled response, but the father answered his own question by volunteering to inform the girl's mother of her whereabouts.

Then the two laid there for a while. The boy shifted over in his bed to make room for his girlfriend to more comfortably lie down. Over the next several hours the boy fell in and out of a restless sleep. Every time he awoke he was comforted by the soft and steady breathing of the girl resting on his chest. The boy quickly learned how to work the morphine machine, and pumped himself full of enough painkiller to wipe out a stable of horses.

After resetting the levels in the drip for a fourth time, Iche asked the boy if he was okay. Not sure how to answer, the boy explained that he was just "in a lot of pain." The male nurse seemed to understand, and cranked the drug levels up to about half as high as the boy had set them. The man then put a finger to his lips, and with a mischievous grin, made his exit.

Chapter 25

Jfer and the boy continued to share a bed for the next week. While the boy was still in the hospital, she refused to leave his side for any reason other than to fulfill her biological needs. After two more nights in the hospital the boy had finally hacked up the last traces of blood in his lungs, and underwent a final checkup. The doctor, a greying man in his early sixties, was very understanding of the boy's pain, and made sure to write out three months of prescription Hydrocodone before allowing him to leave the hospital. The boy planned on taking full monetary and recreational advantage of the pills.

The couple was met with little resistance upon arriving at the boy's home. After protesting for just under an hour, Jfer was given permission to help the boy shower. Mrs. Rivera helped show the girl how to wrap the cast in trash bags, which proved more trouble than they were worth, as water dripped down into the cast as soon as the boy let his arm hang freely. Jfer handled her job efficiently, and had the boy rest his casted arm on the top of the glass panel that made up one wall of the shower cubicle. She then had his body washed and hair shampooed and conditioned within seven minutes flat.

As the boy stepped out of the shower, the girl followed him, leaving the shower running. The boy wrapped a towel around his waist and gave the girl a questioning look.

"Turn the shower off." He said, maintaining his inquisitive expression as the naked girl eagerly tip-toed towards him.

"I figure we have at least ten more minutes before your parents get suspicious of what we're doing in here. Take that towel off." The girl commanded, with a look that made the boy feel stupid for his absence of attraction. In truth, he hadn't been in "the mood" lately for his girlfriend's sexual lifestyle. Even in the hospital, when she had spent both nights in his bed, he had turned down a pity blowjob.

Due to recent events—particularly the ones where he cheated and then killed his friend and only witness—the boy had little confidence his sexual drive would return any time soon. Nonetheless his girlfriend—for now—was now kissing his neck and getting very handsy. He tried to wrap his arms around the girls wet and glistening body, but the plastic-wrapped club on his left arm made the whole attempt feel pathetically awkward. The boy pulled back the arm with the cast and let it hang limply at his side.

"You know I'm not really in the mood right now." Was all the boy could say. He knew Jfer was relieved he was alive, but he couldn't bring himself to touch the girl considering the guilt that weighed heavy on his heart. Instead he turned to leave.

A few minutes later, the boy returned to the den in a T-shirt and gym shorts. As he curled up next to the girl, the boy was struck by the realization that he needed to tell her the truth. It was time. He had no other option. If he didn't tell someone soon it would look like he had tried to kill Adam to keep the secret of his cheating. No, waiting would only prolong the inevitable and make the consequences worse. It was a sickening thought, but the boy decided the girl had every right to know how her friend had really died. He reached the club-arm over his girlfriend to pause Netflix. After a couple jabs at the tiny button, the boy managed to silence the room.

"Need something hon?" Jfer asked, sitting up to look at the boy.

"No. No I'm fine thanks. I uhh, well Jfer I need to tell you the truth about the car crash." The boy stated cautiously, running through the last words quickly.

"You need to tell what?" The girl asked with a stumped look on her face.

The boy then remembered that he had popped three of his new happy-pills already, so his words were naturally slurring. He propped himself up on one elbow, but quickly realized this put too much pressure on his chest to keep himself upright. The boy instead pulled himself up and sat cross-legged facing Jfer.

The last traces of golden evening sun streamed in through the skylight, casting a magical luminescence over the room. The boy felt uncomfortable with just how perfectly romantic the setting was for a heartbreak.

"I need to tell you the truth about the car crash." He stated, clearly pronouncing each word in order to get his point across. The girl understood him this time, but said nothing in response, only stared at him, her face drained of emotion. He could only imagine the thoughts and accusations that churned in the girls head at that very moment.

"I yelled at Adam before we got in the car that night. I was pissed and I popped the edible in my mouth. I was completely sober when we launched over the edge, but I had turned to Adam to apologize and say something when we hit that bend and…" The boy stopped to control his breathing. And prepare himself for what he would say next.

"Why did you get in a fight with Adam? And what were you going to tell him that was so important it distracted you from the road?" Jfer asked. She had a look on her face that said she didn't really want to know the answers to her questions. The boy knew she didn't, and he hesitated for a second, once again considering the alternate route.

Reaching out, the boy took his girlfriend's hand in his own, cast-free hand. He knew he had to do this. He fucked up, and he had to face up to it. Natalie's words rang in the boy's head. He now knew the difference between Natalie and Jfer. The woman understood the consequences of her actions, but she deliberately made the wrong choice despite knowing said consequences. Jfer wasn't like that.

Jfer made the right choice, and if she slipped up at any point, her next set of choices would fix things. The boy had to try and fix things.

"I was yelling at Adam because I was freaking out and he was an open target. I was pissed, and he set me off." The boy made eye contact with the girl to make sure she was following before he continued, maintaining eye contact with his girlfriend, hoping against hope that she would remain his girlfriend after what he was about to do to her.

"Jfer, I wanted to go to that tattoo shop. That one specifically."

The girl looked puzzled.

"I wanted a specific artist. I met her a while back, she's Mr. Jensen's ex-girlfriend."

"Like the math teacher Mr. Jensen?" Jfer questioned suspiciously.

"Yes, not to be confused with Officer Jensen." The boy replied. This elicited a nervous giggle from his girlfriend- not what the boy had wanted.

"Her name is Natalie, I scheduled an appointment a couple weeks ago. After she had finished what you see now." He gestured at his chest, under the blotchy and bruised skin, the wings and family crest could be seen. "She took me up to the roof, and there was a couch, and we smoked a cigarette." His voice quickened. The girl could see where he was going now, and he could see the color drain from her face as she waited for him to keep talking.

"She came on to me. She told me that you and Mr. Jensen didn't matter, and I told her no. She kept pushing though, and I'm sorry." The boy finally dropped his eyes, breaking the eye contact he had held so solidly with the girl in front of him. "I had sex with her. I broke. I'm sorry." The girl began to slowly shake her head in disbelief. Tears began to pool in the corners of her eyes. The girl had shed so many tears already. It killed him to know he was the reason for her continued sorrows.

"After we were done I felt more than guilty. I felt like I was dead inside. I betrayed the one person I loved. I screwed up but I want to fix it."

Now they were both crying. Jfer pulled her hand out of the boy's and used it to muffle the wail of anguish that came from her mouth.

"I was so pissed at myself for making the same FUCKING mistake everyone else makes. I barely remember walking out of the tattoo shop, but Adam knew what had happened and he tried to help. I didn't yell at him because he provoked me. He knew I felt like shit for what I had done. He wanted to help, I saw it on his face." The boy looked up, took a deep breath, and returned his gaze to Jfer. There were no more tears on her side. The girl held the boy's gaze with a cold and angry glare.

"But I flipped out, I exploded on him. I was trying to apologize when we went over the edge. And I was going to ask him how I could fix things with you. But I never got an answer." Finally done with what he had to say, the boy bit his lip and waited. The punishment was clean, quick, and severe.

"Fuck you, Jake Rivera." And with that the girl stood up off the couch and walked out on the boy.

Chapter 26

The boy sat in shock for a moment until the squeak of his front door opening prompted him to move. He was not done yet. He knew Jfer would need him now more than ever, as he would need her. The idea of losing the girl that had opened his eyes to the world terrified him. For once the boy had no words for how he felt. No words to convince the girl to give him a chance. All he had was the tumultuous mix of raw emotions that tore at him, and while he wasn't sure if that was much of a leg to stand on, he would be damned if he let such a special person walk out of his life without a fight.

The boy flew out of the house and saw the girl carefully choosing her steps as she walked down the driveway to the street. She had no car to drive, no gay best friend to pick her up. She stopped at the curb to place her head in her hands. The boy watched in silence for a moment as Jfer's entire world crumbled in front of her. He couldn't handle seeing her shake from sorrow any longer. He wanted to wipe away her tears, not cause them.

"Jfer! I'm sorry!" The boy called out from the stoop.

The girl, startled by his voice, jumped before wiping her eyes, clenching her fists, and turning on the boy.

"It's fine. Really, it is." She said in a calm tone that was betrayed by the fact that she was shouting across the front yard.

"I mean I guess I made you what you are today, being your first girlfriend and making you popular and all." The girl paused. "But hey, you became what you always wanted to be. A cool kid, you fuck over decent girls and bone sluts. Congratulations sir, you have now become a normal, BORING-ASS person. A fucking one amongst millions like you. I thought you were better than that Jake." The girl had tears running down her cheeks by the time she finished.

The boy had nothing to say. The girl was right. He had become a shining example of everything and everyone that he had separated himself from previously in life. The sickest part about it was that he felt a twisted form of satisfaction in becoming the guy he had never been cool enough to be prior to meeting Jfer. She was the one who had started him on the right path. He had been the one who took the wrong turn.

The girl-- sensing the boy's hesitation-- began to slowly back away and turn towards the street. The boy knew this was his one chance to fix things. If he couldn't talk his way back into her loving arms now, he would never again have the chance to.

But nothing came. He had no words. The shock of how selfish and self-indulgent he had been left the boy speechless. And thus was his hell. When he died the boy knew he would be sent to hell, along with most of the snot-nosed pricks of his generation. There he would be forced to relive this moment over and over for eternity. There he would be forced to watch as the girl who opened his heart and taught him how to love walked away. Over and over it would repeat, this one moment in his life would become his torturous eternity.

"Spot!" The boy called after the girl.

She stopped.

The sniffling figure collected herself for a moment and turned around to face the boy, standing under the street-light and crossing her arms for support.

"Excuse me?" The girl said in an attempt at a hostile tone. Her voice quivered most of the way through, but never cracked. She wouldn't give him that.

"I uh, I guess I meant to stay sop. Fuck. Say stop."

"Stop" the girl said with a smirk that cracked her makeup and tear-stained face."

"Wait. I'm going off the dome here trying to say something that can stop you. And all I've got is this." The boy paused to collect his thoughts and took a few cautious steps down the path leading to the driveway. The girl noticed his hesitation and a suspicious look passed over her face, causing the boy to stop in his tracks.

"Fuck it, from the heart then. I love you Jennifer. This isn't about you though."

The girl spit at the ground near the boy's feet.

"Let me finish." He said in a cooing voice.

The girl didn't move, so the boy continued on immediately so as not to ellicit any more suspicion.

"It's not about you. This whole relationship was never about you, it was about me. You showed me a new world. I was like the new kid in town that you wanted to show around. I took advantage of your attention and showed you off. It was a sick fucked up thing because in the end you're right. I became everything that I didn't really want to be."

The boy now had to steady his own voice. The girl in front of him showed no emotion. No hope for him to cling on to and steady himself with. He had to finish his appeal.

"But here's the thing. Along the way I fell in love with all of stupid little shit you do."

The girl slipped a smile as she dropped her head to wipe the tears that came from the corner of her eyes.

"When we first show up to a party, and I knock on the door, you always ring the doorbell too just to make sure 'all the utilities are utilized.'" He air quoted the girl's comment. She took a deep breath and drained the rest of the emotion from her face. The crying had stopped, she was serious now. Luckily the boy had her attention still, so he continued on.

"Actually that's the wrong example. Let me be more to the point. Same situation, we've rang the doorbell and knocked on the door, and now we're waiting for someone to answer. I get anxious waiting there at the door. It's weird, like if the house is quiet, you know?"

The girl was silent, but began to appear impatient.

"You take my hand. Every fucking time we have to wait awkwardly outside someone's front door, only to be judged immediately by everyone in the house as soon as the door opens. You grab four of my fingers and let my thumb hang loose."

The look on the girl's face told the boy he was running out of time. "Which I like." He said with a smile that reached his eyes, something the girl knew was a rarity.

"Because then I can rest my thumb on that stupid little Tiffany ring we found together."

"I found this with Adam." The girl interjected. She gave the boy a look of annoyance and held out her hand, presenting the ring in question under the light.

"Oh." The boy continued with a nervous laugh.

"I like to think we found it together. But that's not the point. The point is, I love the fact that I can rest my thumb on that ring. I love the fact that I have a steady hand to hold as we walk into the party. I love the fact that the gorgeous girl attached to my hip is you. But the idea of forever losing the little things like holding your hand as I walk into a party, or waking up to you sitting cross-legged on the bed in front of me with a bong in hand."

The boy laughed in spite of his own voice, which cracked halfway through "waking". He knew that what he was doing was unconventional. If he really was the guy JFer thought he was then he'd be able to dust himself off after the breakup and hookup with countless girls before breaking down and trying to call her at 3am four months down the line.

"Guys can try and talk their way out of anything, I'm hearing you throw down the word love but I don't think you even know what love is!" The girl said, visibly and verbally getting worked up. "Oh no Mommy and Daddy have marital issues so now I'm allowed to shit all over the idea of love." The girl said in a mocking tone. "Grow the fuck up Jacob. Everyone has mommy and daddy issues these days. That doesn't give them the right to be cold and selfish."

The boy was at a loss for words. He was trying to tap into his emotions but nothing was coming across for the girl.

"No. I'm not shitting on the idea of love, I'm doing my best to try and explain to you that all of this" the boy said, gesturing wildly at himself. "What you say I've turned into; the selfish asshole that prides himself on sleeping around and getting away with it. That's not what I want. I know I can do that. Anybody with a half-decent stroke game and Twitter can do that. Any guy can have a good girl in his life, screw things up somehow, and pretend they don't feel like shit when the girl walks away. I don't want to do that." The boy was running on fumes, he knew there was something deep inside that he was reaching for.

If the girl had been following his word vomit she didn't show it. She was standing perfectly still, shaking her head with a look of frustration.

"It's not about what you want or don't want Jake." The girl took a sharp intake of breath. "Fuck, how many more times can you say 'I' in a conversation?"

And in that moment the memory he had been searching for returned to the boy. Lying in a field next to the girl tripping balls. The boy needed a break in the conversation. Things were going downhill fast, but he knew that his next attempt to display the emotions he felt would be the make-or-break move.

The boy stepped into the grass, still damp from the sprinklers that had soaked it hours earlier. "If it's alright with you I'd like to start my closing argument in the same way my opening argument took place." The boy said to the girl as he lay down on the grass.

He looked straight forward, up into the night sky, and realized in horror that the marine layer made it impossible to see even a single star. It was too late though, the girl was cautiously approaching him. Step by step she closed the distance until she was standing above him.

"I'm a sucker for love stories. Give me your best attempt at Noah Calhoun." JFer said softly before lying down next to the boy.

She didn't take the boy's hand in her own like she had at the park their first night. She did position herself just close enough though for the boy to feel her shoulder pressing against his. He took this as a sign to proceed.

"So, obviously the first time we did this together there were a couple more stars out. But that doesn't matter, there's a huge-ass universe hidden behind that cloudy curtain. We're fucking specks. I know we share this idea because you've said the same thing. All I know is that you're a much brighter speck than I am in the grand scheme of things. I want to grow, learn, and explore new things with you. Because that's what you do, and that's what relationships should be about. This conversation was never about me."

The girl cut him off. "Jake this is about you, you're the one who cheated on me and then killed our best friend."

"Yes I fucked up." The boy paused. Hearing the accusation he feared most from the girl he loved most hurt.

"Okay when you put it that way, I really fucked up. I'm sorry babe, and all I can say is that I let my new-found popularity blow my head up. Now I'll forever live with Adam's death on my conscious. I've accepted that. But you're still lying here next to me, which leads me to believe that there is at least some tiny part of you that wants to give me a second chance. This appeal isn't about me, you already know I messed up- but you also know that I can be a good person."

The boy turned to face the girl. "So what do you want?"

JFer turned to the boy with a look of astonishment. "Now you're trying to bribe me? What the fuck is your problem?"

The boy was sick of the back-and-forth. He sat up, leaned over, and planted a long and steady kiss on the girl's lips.

"I only want you. What do you want?" He asked in a last desperate attempt to save them.

The girl lay quiet for a moment, mulling over the boy's words and his kiss that had once again sparked her heart. "I want you to relax. You just rambled for ten minutes trying to come up with a reason as to why I should take you back. And you came up with "I only want you.""

"Surprisingly it's not very easy to relax when the girl you love and need more than ever is tearing down your proposition for a second chance." The boy said, shifting over so that he was lying on his side facing the girl.

"It's funny." She responded, keeping her eyes locked on the marine layer above her. "And kind of sad, to see how pathetic your try was. But in the end you're right."

"I'm right?" The boy asked in surprise as the girl flipped onto her side to face him.

"You did fuck up."

The boy looked down at the grass between them.

"But you're a good guy Jake, you really are. And in the end I'd rather give a good guy a second chance than try my luck at finding another one."

A smile stretched across the boy's face, and he leaned in to share his smile with the girl..

Chapter 27

"My name is Jake Rivera. I was driving the car that launched off the cliff. It was my poor judgment that killed Adam. I'll carry his death with me for the rest of my life." The boy forced himself to look up from the notecard he had made to keep himself on track. He looked out at the audience that had gathered for his friend's service. He locked eyes first with his girlfriend, who held her chin high despite the grief of the day. Seeing her sit so strong in the face of pain gave the boy enough confidence to turn his attention directly to Adam's parents.

"But there's more than that." A single tear trickled down his cheek. "Adam pulled me out of a lonely place in my life. He was my first best friend. He got me to drop acid on the drop of a dime and showed me a whole new world. Adam opened my eyes to the people and places I had passed every day." The boy's voice strengthened, and he grew more confident as he continued on, desperate to get his message across before the tears came again.

"I'll forever carry Adam's death on my heart. It's an unhealthy burden according to my shrink. But what does he know?" This elicited some scattered laughter. Adam's father smiled and his mother let out a short giggle between her tears.

"I'm okay with carrying Adam's death, because I know it will remind me to carry on his life as well. Adam approached each day with a sense of adventure. He made it his mission to make friends out of every person he came across. He treated every person like a king or queen, he lived in exactly whatever moment and place he had been placed in. And while his life may have been cut short, I know I'll be living the rest of my life meeting new people that had been affected in a positive way by Adam." The tears came. The boy still had three bullet points. He wasn't going to finish. He had to finish. He had to pull something out of his ass to say goodbye to his friend.

Suddenly it came to him. The boy looked out at the audience once more. It consisted of friends and family of Adam, along with the Jensen brothers and the families of Adam's friends.

"Look at this." The boy managed to sputter through the tears. "We're all here because we loved this kid to death." He then turned around, and pulled a cigarette out of his pocket.

"Adam was the coolest kid I knew, and I'll be damned if he goes in the ground without looking cool." With that the boy walked to the coffin, and placed the rolled up tobacco in one of its crevices. He then leaned down and kissed the stained oak box, before turning back to the audience.

All eyes were focused on what he did next. The boy decided to leave things off as Adam would, and with one solid pound on the coffin behind him, he raised his face to the sky and shouted "LONG LIVE THE KING!"